Dear Reader,

The Randall family has become so important to me now. My daughter complains that I talk about them as if they're her cousins! But as their creator, I feel responsible for their happiness, though sometimes they seem to take over. When Abby died in *Randall Honor*, I already knew Russ would get a second chance. I'm so glad it's finally here. He's suffered a long time and I couldn't wait to bring happiness back to him. Isabella is totally different from sweet Abby, but she, too, deserves happiness. And little Angela deserves a good daddy like Russ. But like every couple, Russ and Isabella have to work through a few problems before they can trust each other. Isabella has been taught not to trust a man. And Russ doesn't trust life. By the time they both realize the possibilities, they've worked up their courage to go for it.

Maybe it was because Russ had suffered, or because he didn't believe he could find happiness again. And maybe it was because Isabella didn't expect any happiness for herself. But it was particularly pleasing for me to bring these two lonely people together.

I hope you enjoy their happiness as much as I do. And I hope you remember that happiness can be just around the corner for all of us. If you just believe.

Best,

Judy Christenberry

Dear Reader,

Things get off to a great start this month with another wonderful installment in Cathy Gillen Thacker's series THE DEVERAUX LEGACY. In *Their Instant Baby*, a couple comes together to take care of an adorable infant—and must fight *their* instant attraction. Be sure to look for a brand-new Deveraux story from Cathy when *The Heiress*, a Harlequin single title, is released next March.

Judy Christenberry is also up this month with a story readers have been anxiously awaiting. Yes, Russ Randall does finally get his happy ending in *Randall Wedding*, part of the BRIDES FOR BROTHERS series. We also have *Sassy Cinderella* from Kara Lennox, the concluding story in her memorable series HOW TO MARRY A HARDISON. And rounding out things is *Montana Miracle*, a stranded story with a twist from perennial favorite Mary Anne Wilson.

Next month begins a yearlong celebration as Harlequin American Romance commemorates its twentieth anniversary! We'll have tons of your favorite authors with more of their dynamic stories. And we're also launching a brand-new continuity called MILLIONAIRE, MONTANA that is guaranteed to please. Plus, be on the lookout for details of our fabulous and exciting contest!

Enjoy all we have to offer and come back next month to help us celebrate twenty years of home, heart and happiness!

Sincerely,

Melissa Jeglinski
Associate Senior Editor
Harlequin American Romance

Judy Christenberry

Randall Wedding

TORONTO • NEW YORK • LONDON
AMSTERDAM • PARIS • SYDNEY • HAMBURG
STOCKHOLM • ATHENS • TOKYO • MILAN • MADRID
PRAGUE • WARSAW • BUDAPEST • AUCKLAND

ISBN 0-373-16950-7

RANDALL WEDDING

This edition published by arrangement with Harlequin Books S.A.

Visit us at www.eHarlequin.com

Printed in U.S.A.

ABOUT THE AUTHOR

Judy Christenberry has been writing romances for fifteen years because she loves happy endings as much as her readers do. A former French teacher, Judy now devotes herself to writing full-time. She hopes readers have as much fun reading her stories as she does writing them. She spends her spare time reading, watching her favorite sports teams and keeping track of her two daughters. Judy is a native Texan.

Books by Judy Christenberry

HARLEQUIN AMERICAN ROMANCE

555—FINDING DADDY
579—WHO'S THE DADDY?
612—WANTED: CHRISTMAS MOMMY
626—DADDY ON DEMAND
649—COWBOY CUPID*
653—COWBOY DADDY*
661—COWBOY GROOM*
665—COWBOY SURRENDER*
701—IN PAPA BEAR'S BED
726—A COWBOY AT HEART
735—MY DADDY THE DUKE
744—COWBOY COME HOME*
755—COWBOY SANTA
773—ONE HOT DADDY-TO-BE?†
777—SURPRISE—YOU'RE A DADDY!†
781—DADDY UNKNOWN†
785—THE LAST STUBBORN COWBOY†
802—BABY 2000
817—THE GREAT TEXAS WEDDING BARGAIN†
842—THE $10,000,000 TEXAS WEDDING†
853—PATCHWORK FAMILY
867—RENT A MILLIONAIRE GROOM
878—STRUCK BY THE TEXAS MATCHMAKERS†
885—RANDALL PRIDE*
901—TRIPLET SECRET BABIES
918—RANDALL RICHES*
930—RANDALL HONOR*
950—RANDALL WEDDING*

*Brides for Brothers
†Tots for Texans

THE RANDALLS

Jake ④
m.
B. J. Anderson
- Toby ⑥ m. Elizabeth (son from 1st marriage)
- Caroline
- Josh

Pete ②
m.
Janie Dawson
- Rich ⑦ m. Samantha
- twins
- Russ ⑩ m. Abby (deceased)
- Casey

Brett ③
m.
Anna O'Brien
- Victoria ⑧ m. Jon Wilson
- Jessica

Chad ①
m.
Megan Chase
- Elizabeth ⑥ m. Toby Randall
- Jim
- Drew

THE RANDALL COUSINS

twins separated at birth

Gabriel ⑨
m.
Jennifer Waggoner

Nicholas McMillan ⑨
m.
Sarah Waggoner

Griffin ⑤
m.
Camille Chase
- John
- Melissa

① *Cowboy Cupid*
② *Cowboy Daddy*
③ *Cowboy Groom*
④ *Cowboy Surrender*
⑤ *Cowboy Come Home*
⑥ *Randall Pride*
⑦ *Randall Riches*
⑧ *Randall Honor*
⑨ *Unbreakable Bonds*
⑩ *Randall Wedding*

Chapter One

Russ Randall glanced at his watch. It was only two in the afternoon, but the sun was long gone, buried behind the clouds that had brought the snow. It was early December in Wyoming, and snow wasn't unusual, but this storm had the makings of a fierce blizzard. He hoped he could make it home.

Normally the drive from this point was half an hour, but he'd be lucky if he made it in an hour. The heater was on full force, but he could feel the cold creeping into the truck.

He leaned forward over the steering wheel, pressing for every advantage. Then he slowly hit the brakes, coming to a halt opposite the car sitting at an awkward angle in the ditch. He had to make sure no one was stuck in there before he continued on his way. Ignoring a stranded motorist was like signing his, or her, death warrant.

He undid his seat belt and reached for the door handle just as his passenger door was jerked open. He couldn't even get a word out before a fur-bundled person shoved in a baby carrier and then slammed the door, remaining out in the storm.

"What the...?" Russ began, when he heard a small sound from the carrier. If he'd avoided anything the past year and a half, and he had avoided a lot, he'd avoided babies. Even among his family, no one asked him to hold their babies. They understood.

He heard the same sound again and he peeled back the covering blanket to discover the sweetest face he'd ever seen.

He stared at the beautiful baby. Finally he forced himself to move, reaching for the middle seat belt to strap the carrier in place.

Movement reminded him of the person outside. He zipped up his coat and climbed out of the cab to discover that several suitcases and boxes had been loaded in the back of the truck. He went around his vehicle to the car in the ditch, a Cadillac with New York plates. A couple more boxes were in its open trunk.

He assumed the person was a woman, for she was wrapped in a full-length mink coat and wore a muffler wrapped around her head. He put the rest of the boxes on his truck bed. Then he opened the front passenger door and bundled the woman inside. She seemed to be resisting, but he was anxious to be on his way. The blizzard was worsening.

Once he was back behind the wheel, he opened his coat a little to let in the warmth from the heater. He turned to suggest his passenger do the same and he discovered a beautiful woman, her mink coat shoved off her, her cheeks red with heat, her eyes glittering.

"You're ill!" he exclaimed, recognizing the signs of fever. "Uh, keep your coat on."

"Too hot," she muttered, not looking at him.

"Does the baby need anything?"

"No, Angel's fine."

Russ wasn't going to argue with that. He decided his job was to get these two stranded ladies to town.

He tried to keep focused on his driving, but he couldn't help looking at his passengers occasionally. He'd avoided the company of all women, and in particular babies, the past two years. Abby, his wife, had been pregnant with their child when she died.

He knew he'd never marry again, so he'd never fulfill his dream of children. His family had babies. His twin brother, Rich, and his wife, Samantha, had a little boy. His cousin Toby and his wife, Elizabeth, had two babies. Tori, his cousin and partner in the accounting firm, had a little boy.

He would never have children.

That was why he avoided them. He did his work. That was all there was in his life. He was satisfied with that.

It suddenly occurred to him that he was going to be stuck with the woman and the baby. The town of Rawhide would be shut down, everyone locked safely in their homes. And they wouldn't come out until the storm ended.

Maybe he could make it to the ranch where his parents and aunts and uncles lived. The women there could take care of this lady and her beautiful baby. And they would, if he could get there.

But the ranch was on the other side of Rawhide, a good half-hour drive. Making it there was impossible.

"I need something to drink," she muttered fuzzily.

He took a good look at her. Her fever still seemed high. He thought she was referring to water, but he didn't have any with him. "You'll have to wait just a little while. I'll get you something to drink as soon as we reach town."

She didn't appear to have heard him.

He reached over and felt her face. Lord have mercy, she was on fire! Was he going to have to take her to Jon's? Tori had married Jon Wilson, the new doctor, last year. He'd come to replace Doc, intending to stay only four years. Tori took care of that, he thought with a smile.

Russ caught the shadow of a building through the snow. Had he reached the outskirts of town? Not that Rawhide was big. There was no hotel, not even a motel. They'd had a bed-and-breakfast for a couple of years, but no longer. So he was stuck with his passengers.

He pulled his pickup to a stop right beside the stairs that led up to his apartment over the accounting office he and Tori shared. He drew a deep breath and tried to relax his muscles. Then he said, "We're here."

No response. He lifted the blanket from the baby. He could see the baby breathing, but the infant's eyes remained closed. The woman didn't open her eyes, either. Okay. He couldn't take them both up at once. He'd carry the baby up first and turn on his gas fireplace. The heating was already on, of course.

After he'd released the seat belt, he opened his door and slid out into the storm, the baby carrier sheltered against his chest. He kept a hand on his truck as he went around it. Then he reached out to find the stairs to the apartment. Afraid he'd fall and harm the baby, he kept a tight hold on the banister and climbed slowly.

Once he was inside, he put the carrier on the sofa and crouched down to start the gas fireplace. Then he took the blanket off the top of the carrier. The baby stirred, but then settled down again. He was relieved.

He left the baby and headed out into the storm again. When he got to the bottom of the stairs, he opened the passenger door of the truck. "Lady, you're going to have to help me. Are you awake?" he yelled over the storm. He pulled the mink coat back on her shoulders and fastened the hook.

She accepted the coat, but as he pulled her out, she lay her head on his shoulder and closed her eyes. "Lady, we've got to get upstairs to the baby. Come on. Hold on to me. We'll be fine."

Despite his request, she wasn't much help. But they eventually reached the top of the stairs. He dragged her the few steps to the front door and opened it, then got her to the sofa and lowered her to the cushions. He felt her face again and headed to the small kitchen for some pain reliever and water.

After giving her the pain reliever and some water, he moved the baby carrier and let the woman lie down on the sofa. He covered her with the mink coat. The baby opened its eyes and suddenly let out a yell.

"So, we're hearing from you, are we?" He stared at the baby, not sure what to do for her. "Hmm, Mom said your name is Angel. That would make you a girl, wouldn't it?"

Of course, he received no answer, though the baby continued to scream. He'd thought the mother had passed out, but she pushed herself up and reached for the baby. "Whoa!" Russ said. "You can't go anywhere. What do I do for the baby? Change her diaper? Feed her?"

"Bottle," she mumbled.

"Where is it? In the back of the truck?"

She turned to look at him. "I...I don't know."

"In the boxes? We loaded boxes from your car in the back of my truck."

"Yes. I...I think so."

He zipped up his coat and pulled on his gloves and hat. "Stay under your coat and relax," he said. Then he hurried out into the storm again, which showed no indication of letting up. He grabbed two boxes. One was diapers, the other appeared to contain bottles. He carried them up the stairs and set them inside. The baby was crying, but the woman was sleeping. He made two more trips, bringing up the suitcases and a third box.

Each time he entered, the baby was still yelling and the woman still sleeping.

He opened the box labeled ''feeding system.'' Fortunately there were instructions that were fairly easy to follow. He put the milk mixture in the microwave and heated it for the time given. Then he put the nipple on it and shook it. He felt like a pro when he tested it on his arm the way he'd seen his mother do.

''Okay, baby, I think it's ready. You want to try?''

He stuck the nipple in the little mouth, which instantly clamped on. He held the bottle with one hand and unfastened the straps holding the baby in the carrier. He should pick her up, shouldn't he? Then he reached for the phone, leaving her in the carrier. He dialed a number with one hand, knowing it by memory.

''Mom?'' he replied to the voice he heard. He was lucky that one of the women on the ranch answered.

''I've been wondering about you, Russ,'' Janie, his mother, said. ''I called half an hour ago.''

''I know, but I just got in. I have a problem. Do you pick up a baby when you're feeding it?''

Janie remained silent, apparently stunned by his question. Finally she said, "You have a baby?"

"I picked one up on the highway with her mother. The mother is passed out with a high fever. The baby was screaming. I followed directions and fixed the bottle and she's eating, but—"

"How old is the baby?"

"I'm not sure, but she's really little."

"A girl?"

"I think so. Her mother said her name is Angel."

"You haven't changed her diaper?"

"No. Should I do that?"

"Yes. Halfway through the bottle, burp her on your shoulder. Then change her diaper. Then finish feeding her and burp her again."

"Okay," he said, staring at the baby. Then he said, "Thanks, Mom."

"Wait! Don't hang up. Is there anything I can do? Do you want your father to drive me into town?"

"No! The storm's really bad and it's not ending anytime soon. I'll call you later when I get this feeding taken care of."

"Okay, dear. I'm proud of you."

Russ shook his head. He hadn't done anything to make his mother proud. Anyone would've figured out how to feed that screaming machine. He put the phone down and pulled the bottle out of Angel's mouth. Immediately the screaming started again. "Baby, you've got a siren like I've never heard."

He shrugged out of his jacket, then picked up the

baby. That change of behavior startled the baby and she took a breath. Any hope she was going to stop screaming disappeared, however. He put her on his shoulder and patted her back. She continued to cry, but it wasn't nonstop.

Her mother stirred and Russ didn't know what to do. Then a large burp ripped out of the baby. He drew her down from his shoulder, staring at her. This delicate little bundle had made that sound? He hurriedly laid her down on the carpet and grabbed the box of diapers. Then he undid the sleeper and undid the tapes on the diaper.

''Ooh! Definitely ripe, young lady.'' He set the dirty diaper aside and spread out the fresh one. It wasn't too hard to figure out. Finding the right snaps on the pajamas was more difficult. Especially when she continued to scream. He quickly offered the bottle again.

Peace! Her mother stopped trying to get up, now that the baby had stopped screaming. Russ felt as if he'd scored a real success. When the baby got close to the end of the bottle, its little rosebud mouth stopped working. He eased the bottle back, and the little jaws started working again. The third time the baby didn't move. He thought about skipping the burping again, but he was afraid that would harm the baby. So he put her on his shoulder and burped her again.

This time, after burping, she fell asleep and remained asleep. With relief, he put her in the carrier and covered her with the blanket.

For the first time since he'd picked them up, Russ could take a minute for himself. Then he felt the woman's face. It was still hot, but not as hot as earlier. He picked up the phone again.

"Dr. Wilson," Jon said when he answered.

"Jon, it's Russ."

"Hey, you doing all right? Some storm, huh?"

"Yes. I picked up a stranded woman and her baby on the road. I managed to feed the baby and she's sleeping fine. But the woman is very hot. I got some pain relievers and a little water down her, but is there anything else I need to do?"

"Did you put her in bed?"

"No, she's on the sofa, but I can do that. I'm using her mink coat as cover right now."

"She'd be better off if she was in bed with regular covers on her. She may get overheated under the fur. What's her temperature?"

"I don't know. It's come down a little since I gave her the medicine, but she's still hot. I don't see any rash or anything. I don't know how long they were stuck out there, either."

"It's hard for me to say without examining her. But do you have some soup? Preferably chicken, or beef consommé you could heat up and feed her?"

"I'll check. Okay. Put her in bed and feed her soup. Anything else?"

"All the liquids you can get down her. Clear liquids, like juice."

"Okay. If you don't mind, I may call you later if that doesn't work."

"Of course, Russ. Call if you have any questions. Is the baby all right?"

"Well, she's got the healthiest lungs I've ever heard. But she's sleeping just fine now." Russ started to hang up, but then he thought of another question. "Hey, how often does she take a bottle?"

"How big is she?"

"Tiny."

"Probably every four hours. Don't wake her. I'm sure she'll wake you up when she's ready to eat. Did you change her diaper?"

"Yeah. Okay, I'll see what I can do for the mom before the baby gets hungry again."

"Good job, Russ."

Russ wasn't used to all the praise coming his way today. He was only doing what he had to do. He shoved those thoughts away and reached for the largest suitcase. He found a pair of silk pajamas in forest-green. He looked at them and then at the woman. They looked conservative enough. He carried them into his bathroom. Then he turned down the king-size bed.

He returned to the couch and pulled off the mink coat. "C-c-cold," she muttered, not opening her eyes.

"Come on, lady. You've got to put on your pajamas and go to the bathroom. Then I'll put you to bed."

She didn't respond.

He had no idea what her name was. He bent over

her. ''Lady, what's your name? Come on, wake up. What's your name?''

''Izzy.''

She still didn't open her eyes. And he wasn't sure what that name was. ''Izzy? Izzy, open your eyes.''

Long lashes fluttered several times. Then they settled on her cheeks again.

''No, Izzy, come on, open your eyes.'' He pulled on her arms, raising her to a sitting position as she struggled to wake up. ''Izzy, I'm going to help you to the bathroom, okay? When you get in there, put on your pajamas. Okay?''

He slid an arm around her slender figure and lifted her to her feet. ''Come on, Izzy. I'm going to feel pretty strange if that's not your name.''

They made their way to his bathroom. ''Izzy, you're in the bathroom now. Can you change your clothes?'' When she started to undress, he slipped out of the room.

He came back after putting a pan on the stove and filling it with a can of chicken soup. He knocked on the door. ''Izzy? Are you dressed in your pajamas?''

When there was no answer, he eased the door open. No, she wasn't in her pajamas. She was sitting on the floor half-asleep. He took a deep breath and got her pajama bottoms on her. Then he carried her to the bed. He removed her sweater. She was a beautiful woman, and Russ held his breath, trying not to notice. By the time he got her into the pajama top, he was breathing heavily. He pulled the covers over her and was relieved when her eyes closed and she didn't move.

He went back to the stove and poured the soup into a bowl. Then he poured some grape juice into a glass. Once again, he tried to wake Izzy. After propping her up on several pillows, he managed to feed her a few spoonfuls of soup. Then a few drops of juice. Not much.

Finally he let her sleep.

It was his turn. He took out a frozen dinner and put it in the microwave. It was well past lunchtime and he was hungry. After he'd fed himself, he lay down on the sofa and decided he'd rest a few minutes.

He awoke to the "siren" sounding for the baby's next meal. He'd meant to have a bottle ready so the baby wouldn't wake her mother.

Too late.

How in the hell had nature chosen him to be a nursery maid? That was the last thing he wanted to do, but at this point he had no choice. He steeled himself to pick up the warm bundle of baby, fighting the joy that flowed through him. He was in big trouble.

Chapter Two

Forty-eight hours.

Russ stared at the white world outside his window. Because of a snowstorm, he was lost.

Not lost in the snow. He was lost in a baby's warmth. In her tenderness. In her need for an adult to care for her. Every four hours, she signaled her need clearly, but her mother couldn't respond. Oh, she tried. He'd been amazed how she'd stir from the deepest sleep to try to get to her baby. Every time he'd assured her he'd take care of Angel.

He was becoming an expert with the tiny baby. He could even get her to stop screaming—at least for a minute or two—before the bottle was ready.

She recognized his voice, his touch. She knew when he showed up, food would soon follow. But this afternoon, they'd varied their routine.

Izzy had begged to feed her baby. To hold her against her. She hadn't run a fever in a while, but she was still weak. When he used that excuse, she'd promised to stay on the bed if he'd bring the baby to her. So he'd done so.

He'd had to leave the room, because it hurt too much to let someone else feed her. In forty-eight hours, Angel had carved a place in his heart.

He stood there, staring at the blizzard, telling himself that he was foolish even to think of a relationship with Angel. For all he knew, Angel had a perfectly upstanding, caring father. Izzy had said nothing about their reason for being on the road alone. He didn't even know their destination. They could've been taking the scenic route to Yellowstone.

He gave a grim smile at that thought. Not where he'd take a new baby. Hard to be interested in mountains and hot springs when your kid was waking you up every four hours. His brothers and friends had mentioned how tired you got when you couldn't sleep straight through the night.

He loved getting up with Angel. But he was wearing down, he had to admit.

''Hello?'' Izzy called from the bedroom. Russ realized he'd never told her his name.

He hurried into the bedroom, his hands reaching out to take the baby.

''Hi. I…I need a clean diaper.''

Her eyes, just as blue as Angel's, weren't glittery with fever any longer. Her black hair hung down her back in tangled curls, and her pajama top was almost slipping off her slender shoulders. He thought her face was a little gaunter than it had been when she was running a fever.

"I can change her. I've gotten quite good at it in the past couple of days."

"I'm sure you have," she said softly, smiling shyly. "I don't know how to thank you."

He tried to resist the warmth and charm. "No need." He held out his hands for the baby again.

"She needs a new nightgown. If you'll bring me one..."

"I'll take care of it," he said firmly, and scooped Angel into his arms. Then he hurried out into the living room.

He'd made part of the sofa into a changing table. He lay Angel down on the soft blanket he'd spread out. "I just stole you from your Mommy, didn't I, little girl. But I missed you. Did you drink all your milk? What a good girl you are," he added, smiling at her. He was crooning nonsense to her, and she loved it, as usual.

She was too young to smile at him, he'd decided, but she put those rosebud lips together and tried to blow bubbles. "Did you miss me? Did you think I'd gone away? Of course not."

He gently removed her nightgown. Pretty soon he'd need to wash a load of baby clothes. Would his regular laundry soap be all right? He'd have to call his mom again. Not that she'd mind. She seemed to be enjoying his calls.

He changed her diaper and found another soft nightgown, this one pink, instead of a blue print.

"Pink is your color, my Angel. It makes you look beautiful. You've got your mother's hair, of course." It was black and curly, making her look like an expensive doll. He could imagine her in her terrible twos, those curls bouncing in every direction as she raced through the house, getting into trouble.

To his surprise, the picture was as clear as could be. Much clearer than his memories of Abby. He stared at the baby in horror. What was wrong with him? This baby wasn't his. Abby was his. His memory, his love.

Angel's face puckered up, as if he'd frightened her. Abby would never want that. Russ relaxed once more, using his soothing voice to reassure the child.

"Hello?" called Izzy. "Has she gone to sleep?"

He still hadn't told Izzy his name. "Just a minute," he called back. Then he picked up Angel and walked to the door of the bedroom. "She's settling down now. I've been letting her sleep in the carrier. Is that all right?"

"Yes, of course, but if you put her here, I can feed her when she wakes up."

"Not unless you get up and make a bottle."

He felt badly about his abrupt return to reality. She bit her bottom lip. "Maybe I can manage that, too."

"I apologize, Izzy. What in hell is that short for, anyway?"

"Isabella."

"Oh. That's a lovely name. I'll go put Angel to bed. Then I'll come back and introduce myself." That was the least he could do. It looked as if she was finally getting well. He'd talked to Jon several times to make sure he was doing the right thing.

He laid the baby in the carrier and tucked a blanket around her, thinking he'd never seen anything quite as beautiful as Angel sleeping. The phone rang and he hurried to answer it so it wouldn't wake the baby.

"Hi, son. It's Mom. Everyone is waiting for our daily report. How's the baby doing?"

He chuckled. "*I'm* doing fine, Mom, thank you for asking."

"Well, I can tell that. Now, how's the baby?"

"Doing fine, too. She just finished her bottle, had a change of clothes and has gone back to sleep."

"You're doing a wonderful job," Janie said.

"Well, her mother fed her just now. I guess she should get some praise, too."

"The mother's awake? How is she doing?"

"I think she's better. I was just going to fix her something to eat. Why don't I call you back after she eats?"

"All right. Ask her—"

"I know what to ask her. Talk to you later."

He'd fed the woman soup ever since they'd been in his apartment, but he didn't think she'd finished as much as a can. He stepped to the door of the bedroom. "Isabella, I'm going to make an omelette and share it with you. I'll be back in a minute."

A faint thank-you drifted after him as he headed for the kitchen. He concentrated on the omelette, able to handle that with no trouble. He wondered about the woman, was not even sure she was a good mother. After all, she and her baby had been alone in a storm.

Of course, the storm had come up suddenly. Even the weatherman hadn't given them much warning. Nevertheless he'd warn her to check more carefully before she set out again.

He made a vegetable and cheese omelette. Once he made sure she would eat meat, he'd fix her a steak. But he thought this would go down easier for her first real meal. He cut about a fourth of the omelette for her. Then he put the rest on his plate.

He dug out a tray and put both plates on it. Then he added some orange juice and some buttered toast. That should be enough for her first meal.

He entered the bedroom to find her eyes closed. Going to the opposite side of the bed, he set down the tray. Then he leaned over the bed and shook her shoulder. "Isabella? Wake up. I've brought you some lunch."

She blinked several times, staring at him. Again he was reminded of how much Angel's eyes were like her mother's. "I...don't think I can keep anything down."

"Just try a little bit. You won't get stronger until you eat something."

She struggled to sit up against the pillows and he shoved another pillow behind her. Her fingers were trembling and she grabbed them to try to hide her weakness.

"Do I need to feed you?"

"No! No, I'm s-sure I can manage."

But when she picked up the fork and it shook, he realized he shouldn't have asked. "This time I'll feed you. I don't want you getting my pajama top dirty," he added with a smile.

Unfortunately that apparently reminded her of a question she wanted to ask. "Why am I wearing your pajamas?"

"I wasn't sure how to wash silk pajamas." He scooped up a bite of egg, cheese and veggies and held it in front of her.

"I have nightgowns in my suitcase," she said, not taking the bite.

"Come on before I drop it." He was pleased when she opened her mouth. She chewed slowly, but it didn't come back out. That made him think he'd been successful.

"It's very good, but—"

"By the way, I apologize. My name is Russ. Russ Randall."

She stared at him. "Randall? I've heard that name before."

He held up another bite. ''Try another bite before it gets cold.''

''But...'' she began, but then stopped talking. He assumed she was following directions and carefully shoved the bite into her mouth.

She covered her mouth with her hand. ''Did you bring a napkin?'' she muttered after a minute.

He handed her the small glass of juice. ''Drink some juice and I'll go get napkins.''

When he returned, he decided her drink of juice must've been small. The level hadn't gone down much. ''Take another swallow.''

She lifted the glass to her lips, but didn't drink much. ''I remember where I heard your name.''

''Oh, really? Where? Connected to rodeos?''

She appeared surprised by the question. ''No. I don't know anything about rodeos.''

''Really? That's a switch. I thought maybe you'd heard of Pete, Toby or Rich.''

''Who are they?''

''Randalls who've made a name for themselves.''

He held up another bite and she took it. ''This really is good, Russ.''

''Thanks. Want some toast?''

She took the toast and bit off a little.

He fed her more. She started to speak, but he gave her a determined stare, and she took the bite.

''Didn't you make a name for yourself?'' she asked.

"Not as a rodeo cowboy. I'm an accountant. Not exactly headline stuff." He'd always scored a lot lower than the rest of his family with the ladies. Somehow, adding up numbers wasn't as exciting as wrestling bulls or riding bucking broncos. Of course, he didn't suffer broken bones, either. Rich had done that. But it was how he met Samantha, so maybe it was worth it.

"Accountants are very important," Isabella said solemnly.

He thought she was mocking him, but her look was sincere.

"You're serious?"

"Of course. Accountants run the world."

"Well, they certainly keep count of everything." He scooped up more egg.

"No! I'll just nibble on my toast and drink more juice. I don't think I should try too much too soon."

Russ frowned. "But you only had a few bites."

"But they were big bites. Besides, your share will get cold if you don't eat some of it soon."

"All right. But let me know if you want more."

She smiled in agreement and picked up her toast.

Russ took a bite of omelette. Lunch was a bit late today and he was hungry.

"How many brothers do you have?"

He looked up, surprised by her question. "Two."

"But you named three, Pete, Toby and Rich."

"Only Rich is my brother. My twin, to be exact. Pete's my dad and Toby's a cousin. I've got another brother, Casey. He's the baby of the family. Well, that's not true. He's the baby of this generation, but we've got three babies in the next generation.''

She stared at him. ''How many people are in your family?''

''Well, my father is one of four Randall brothers. They all married and had eleven children between them. Then there's Griffin—he's a cousin—and his wife Camille, who have two kids. Then there's Gabe and Nick, two more cousins, also twins. Gabe and his wife Sarah just had twins and Nick and his wife are expecting. I think that makes a total of twenty-nine and growing. We're a big family.''

That's when Russ discovered she'd fallen asleep. Obviously his family wasn't as dynamic as he thought.

He eased himself off the bed and carried the tray to the kitchen. He didn't get her to eat much, although in addition to the bit of omelette, she'd managed half a piece of toast and half a glass of juice. Maybe he'd better check with Jon.

When his cousin-in-law answered the phone, he asked him if that was enough food for one meal.

''Sounds like it. Unless you make really bad omelettes,'' he teased.

''They're my specialty, Jon.''

He heard Tori protesting behind her husband. Omelettes had been Abby's thing for him to fix her, especially if she was sick.

''Russ, I'm sorry. I—''

"Don't worry about it, Jon. She did eat half a piece of toast and drank half a glass of orange juice."

"Big glass?"

"No, a juice glass."

"That's probably best. If she keeps that down, that's good."

"You mean she might not?"

"You never know."

"Man, that's not something to look forward to."

"Nope. That's why I keep nurses around." Jon chuckled, but then he asked, "Hey, did you find out anything about your mystery guest?"

"Her name is Isabella."

"Pretty name." He had to repeat it for Tori. "So, I guess she's Italian."

"That would be a good guess. She has long black curls."

"Is she a teenage runaway?"

Russ paused. "No, I don't think so. I'd guess she's in her mid-twenties."

"So what else did she tell you?"

"Uh, that's it. I was busy trying to get her to eat. That seemed more important than pumping her for information." He knew he sounded stiff. But he felt awkward once he realized what a poor job he'd done. Man, he certainly didn't want to call his mother now.

"I'm sure Isabella will tell you anything you want to know when she feels better," Jon said soothingly, reminding Russ of how he talked to Angel.

"Yeah. Well, I'd better go. Mom's still waiting for her daily report."

"Tori talked to her mother yesterday. The whole bunch of parents are gathering for your daily report."

"Must be because of the blizzard. Not much to do when you're trapped in the house."

"Right. Well, call me if you have any concerns. Oh, I heard the weather report a short while ago. They think the storm might blow itself out by tomorrow afternoon."

"Terrific," Russ said, but he noticed a decided lack of enthusiasm in himself that he didn't want to examine.

"Okay, we'll talk to you later."

"Yeah. Thanks, Jon."

Could he put off calling his mother? The four sets of parents all lived together in the main ranch house. They shared their problems and their joys with one another. The kids all grew up together. He was as close to his cousins as he was to Casey. He'd admit he was a little closer to Rich, since they were identical twins, but not much.

They were all one big happy family.

Until Abby died.

Then he'd bowed out. Oh, he'd still been a member of the family, but he'd avoided all their big get-togethers. He'd avoided every rodeo they had at the ranch. He'd withdrawn into a colorless world where he didn't have to risk dealing with his emotions.

He'd known it was cowardly of him. But he couldn't bear the pain of the memories. The sight of the joy his brother or cousins felt with their new babies. The soft touches, the exchanged looks with their wives. He'd shared all that with Abby. But no more.

He'd fallen into a rut of nothingness.

Okay, so now it was time to reenter life. His fingers actually shook as he picked up the phone. He could start slowly. After Isabella and Angel went on their way, he could attend a few family functions. That would do for a while.

He dialed the number, and Red, the man who'd taken care of the house for the past forty years, answered.

"Hey, boy, you making it all right?"

"Sure, Red. But I can't quite make biscuits as light as yours," Russ teased.

"It's in the wrist, boy. You know that."

Russ chuckled and asked for his mother.

"She's been waitin' for your call."

"Russ?" his mother asked when she got on the line. "Did she wake up?"

"Yeah, she did, but not for long. And she was pretty weak. I fixed her some food, but she didn't eat much."

"What did you fix her? An omelette?"

He should've known his mother would guess that. ''Yeah.''

''Oh, good. That would be good for her.''

''I hope so. Her name is Isabella, but that's all I learned. She fell asleep too quickly.''

''Oh, my. She must be really weak.''

''Yeah. I don't know how long she was sick before I found them.''

''How's Angel?''

''As beautiful as ever. She recognizes my voice now.'' He regretted adding that information.

''Uh, yes, babies do that quickly. So her mother's name is Isabella? That sounds Italian.''

''That's what Jon said.''

''I wonder if she was coming here to visit someone? We have a few Italian families around here.''

''Probably not, Mom. I think she would've told me at once. But I'll admit she's not thinking too clearly. She fell asleep while I was explaining our family to her.''

Janie laughed. ''No wonder. There's so many of us.''

''I know. But she'd heard our name before.''

''Well, that happens with Pete and Toby and even Rich.''

It bothered Russ how much he was pleased to be able to tell his mother that she'd never heard of anyone connected with the rodeo. ''No, she hadn't heard of them. She's from New York, you know. At least, her license plates say New York.''

"Oh. Then I wonder how—"

"I don't know, Mom. I'll try to ask her the next time she wakes up. But I've got to go get the kitchen cleaned up right now. Before Angel's next meal."

"Of course, son. Oh, the snow is supposed to end tomorrow. We'll get in to see how you're doing as soon as we can."

"Thanks, Mom, but there's no hurry."

When he hung up the phone, he stood there, his hand on the receiver, wishing everyone would quit telling him about the end of the blizzard. As if that was a good thing.

Chapter Three

When he moved to the kitchen to clean it up, he first took two steaks out of the freezer. A little steak and some vegetables would be good for Isabella. He'd cook them after Angel's six-o'clock feeding.

He checked on Isabella several times before Angel finally sounded the alarm. He listened for Isabella to ask to feed her baby again, but he heard nothing. He gathered the baby against his chest and put the bottle in her mouth and all noise ceased. He cooed to her, entertaining her while she ate. Entertaining himself. He warned himself not to depend on Angel's being around. After all, the snowstorm was supposed to end tomorrow.

But he doubted Isabella would have the strength by then to move on. After all, four bites of an omelette had knocked her out. It was strange that she hadn't even stirred when Angel woke up. Suddenly he panicked. Still holding Angel, he jumped up from the couch and hurried to the bedroom door.

But Isabella was fine. She was curled under the

covers, sound asleep and seemingly at peace. He backed away before Angel's greedy guzzling of her bottle could bother her mother. Was Isabella going to sleep through dinner, too?

He'd looked forward to eating with Isabella. How pathetic. He was looking forward to dinner with a woman just this side of a coma. Yeah, he was going to have to change his lifestyle. Get out more. He didn't need to consider dating or anything like that. He had no intention of dating. But he could hang out with his family.

It was just that he was curious about Isabella and Angel. He wanted to know they would be all right. That they had someone to turn to.

She probably had a truckload of relatives anxious to know what had happened to her. Especially if her car and her coat indicated her level of income. A runaway wouldn't leave in her full-length mink coat and the Cadillac. That was a silly idea.

He had Angel changed and back down asleep before he heard anything from the bedroom. A thump. He hurried to the door and saw nothing. Including no one in the bed. He turned to the bathroom, but the door was open and the room was empty. He turned back to the bed and saw Isabella sprawled out on the floor beside it.

''Isabella! What happened?''

''I need to go to the bathroom,'' she whispered.

He lifted her from the floor and helped her to the bathroom. Once he got her inside, he stood her against the sink.

"Can you manage on your own?"

"Yes."

He wasn't sure it was wise to leave her there alone, but he didn't want to embarrass her. He'd already seen more of her than he wanted her to know.

He hovered outside the door, waiting for her to call him.

"Russ?"

He barely heard her. Had the omelet made her worse?

He opened the door and found her where he'd left her. "Did you take care of business?"

She nodded. He scooped her up into his arms and maneuvered her through the door. When he got her back to the bed, he followed her down to the side of the bed. "Are you hurting anywhere?"

She shook her head.

"But you seem more out of it than before," he said, really worried.

"Sleepy," she muttered.

He pulled the cover over her shoulders. "But I was going to cook you dinner. Aren't you hungry?"

"Sleepy," she repeated.

He left the room and grabbed the phone to call Jon again. Tori answered this time.

"Hi, Russ. Is everything all right?"

"I don't know, Tori. She never really got awake. I found her on the floor because she fell trying to get to the bathroom. I got her in there and left her alone for a few minutes. Then she called me and wanted to go back to bed. All she'd say was she was sleepy. I was going to cook her supper, but she's gone back to sleep. Does that sound normal?"

His cousin repeated the facts to Jon, her husband. He took the phone. "Does she seem to be sleeping okay?"

"Yeah, her breathing is even. Actually, she seems to be sleeping more deeply."

"Probably she didn't get any good sleep until you got more food down her. I bet the next time she wakes up, she'll be hungry. Don't worry, Russ."

"Whatever you say, Jon." He knew he didn't sound satisfied with Jon's words, but he couldn't help worrying.

"If you get worried later, give us a call. No matter what the time."

"Okay, thanks. Hopefully I won't have to bother you."

Russ went back into the bedroom. He stared down at Isabella, watching her breathe. Then he walked out to the living room and looked at Angel. They were both sleeping fine. Maybe if he watched *Monday Night Football* he could forget the warmth and beauty of the two females. But he knew Angel had already claimed his heart. What worried him even more was that Isabella had that effect on him, too. He couldn't feel anything for her! Could he?

WHEN SHE WOKE UP Isabella had no idea where she was. She realized she must have been ill, because she was very shaky. What had woken her up?

It had to be Angel, of course. But had she stopped crying? That didn't sound like Angel. She usually screamed continuously until she got her bottle. They'd been in a hotel. Was that where—? She heard a man's voice.

She struggled from the big bed and managed to get as far as the door, leaning against the wall for support. She silently opened the door and stared into the next room.

There was her child, wrapped in a blanket and snuggled against a man's bare chest, taking her bottle. Isabella watched as the man moved around the room, as if slowly waltzing with Angel. He was wearing loose sweatpants, hanging low on his hips—and nothing else.

"Who are you?" she demanded, but her voice came out faint and weak.

"Isabella! You're up!"

"You know me?"

He gave her a strange look. "We introduced ourselves last night. Don't you remember?"

"No. Where am I?"

He moved closer and she almost fell over. "I think you'd better get back in bed. Angel and I will come in there and we'll talk while she finishes her bottle." He bent over and got a clean nightgown and diaper before coming toward her.

She stumbled back to bed, already exhausted by the brief exchange. As she pulled the cover up, she realized she had nothing on her legs. She was only wearing a pajama top and panties. Her panties, someone else's top.

The man sat on the foot of the bed, still feeding the baby. "I picked the two of you up three days ago on the road south of Rawhide. A blizzard was starting and I was trying to make it back to Rawhide. Your car was off the road in the ditch."

She didn't remember any of this. Three days ago?

"You opened my passenger door before I could get out and shoved in Angel in her carrier. Then you started loading your suitcases and boxes. I climbed out and helped you. Then I got you in the truck and myself behind the wheel. When I looked at you, I realized you were running a high fever.

"We got back here and I brought you both up here and started taking care of you." He stood and went over to the curtains. He pulled them open and showed her a white nothingness. He pulled the curtain closed again. "Helps keep the cold out."

"You mean the snow is as high as the second story?"

"No. But with a storm, we get a lot of wind. Until it blows itself into North Dakota, there's more snow in the air than there is on the ground. Travel is impossible."

"Oh. So we're in Rawhide?"

"Yeah. Where were you heading?"

"Rawhide."

He stared at her as if she'd said something strange. "You were?"

"Yes. Is there something wrong with that? Don't you get visitors in Rawhide?" She shifted under the covers, feeling uneasy suddenly.

"Yeah, sure. Were you visiting someone?"

"Yes, my aunt."

"Oh, that explains it. But Angel is too young to be traveling. And you need to watch the weather closely in Wyoming."

"Thanks for the warning!" she snapped angrily, but she was so weak her eyes filled with tears.

"Hey, no need to cry. I saved you."

"I'm sure we would've been all right," she said with a sniff.

He stared at her. "No. You would've frozen to death."

His raw statement made everything worse. "Give me my baby!"

"Why? She needs to be changed so she can go back to sleep."

"I know that! I can take care of her!"

"Can you? You can barely stand. You certainly can't carry her around, and you've been very sick. I don't think you should push it."

She gave up, though she didn't think it was her nature. But he was right. She didn't have any strength. She turned over and buried her face in a soft pillow. "Go away!"

She heard him stand and walk away. When she looked up she was alone again, the door closed.

Wearily, she pushed her hair back from her face and tried to think about her next step. But it seemed too hard to make a decision. Gradually her lashes lowered over her eyes.

AFTER A SLEEPY Angel was settled back down in her carrier, Russ silently opened the door of his bedroom and discovered Isabella had gone back to sleep.

He breathed a sigh of relief. Last night she'd seemed sweet and cooperative. This morning she was difficult...except that she was too weak. He really needed to feed her again, but he was thinking they both might benefit from another couple of hours' sleep. This was Angel's six-o'clock feeding.

He returned to the air mattress he used when he went camping. It was better than the floor. He was too old to sleep on the floor. Okay, he wasn't ancient, only in his early thirties, but he felt older.

He lay down, thinking of his king-size bed in the next room. He had a second bedroom, but he'd made it into an office. There was no bed there. One thing about taking care of Angel, though. He didn't have to worry about falling to sleep.

That was true this morning, too.

AROUND EIGHT, Russ pulled on jeans and a sweater, using the spare bathroom. Then he headed for the kitchen. He first put on a pot of coffee. Then he put oatmeal on to cook. He fried bacon and added buttered toast. When it was all ready, he went to the bedroom door and opened it.

"Isabella, I'm serving breakfast in five minutes. Want to visit the bathroom beforehand?"

At least she'd opened her eyes. She stared at him, blinking several times.

Then she nodded and began shoving back the cover. Until she reached her bare legs. "I don't have anything to wear."

"That top comes almost to your knees. Come on. If we don't hurry, the bacon will burn." He noticed interest in her eyes when he mentioned bacon. That was a good sign. He helped her to the bathroom.

When he had her back in bed, he went to the kitchen and loaded the tray with their breakfasts and came back. He walked around the bed and piled the pillows behind her so she was almost sitting up. Then he slid the tray closer.

"Help yourself," he said, picking up the bowl with the most oatmeal. She picked up her own bowl, but she stared at him.

"I like my oatmeal with a little sugar," he said, sprinkling it on his cereal, "and then I add raisins. Does that suit you?"

She nodded and he added sugar and raisins for her.

"Want some milk to cool it off?"

She nodded again. He poured some for her. "Can you stir it up yourself?"

She nodded. Good thing he didn't expect a lot of conversation.

"Eat a piece of bacon and a bite of toast while it cools," he ordered. He figured if he gave her a choice, she'd refuse everything. She followed his lead. In fact, she ate half a piece of toast. Then he started eating the oatmeal and she followed suit.

Fifteen minutes later, the tray was pretty much emptied. He'd eaten most of it, but she'd done a pretty good job. "Feel better?"

She nodded again.

"Are you ever going to speak again?"

"Thank you for breakfast."

"You're welcome. Now, who were you coming to visit? They'll be worried about you."

"No. She didn't know I was coming."

"Then whoever you left will be worried. Tell me who to call and I'll let them know you're all right."

She said nothing.

"What's going on here? Why aren't you talking?"

"Because there's no one I want to tell."

"You came from New York?"

"How did you know that?" she asked, stiffening.

He smiled as he shook his head. She was a suspicious woman. "I saw your license plate."

"Oh."

He'd told Jon he didn't think she was a runaway, but now he wondered. "Are you hiding from someone?"

"What if I am? I'm an adult."

"I don't think that's an adult way to handle things."

''Well, I think it is. I'm too weak right now to fight. When I'm strong again, I'll handle everything.''

She was already tiring, and he wanted more information before she went back to sleep. ''Who is Angel's father?''

''Timothy Walker, my...my husband.''

''Where is he?''

''He's dead.''

Russ knew the elation that filled him was wrong. And it didn't mean he could keep Angel, but at least for now, he was the only man in her short life. ''When did he die?''

''Six months ago.''

''Angel looks about a month old. So you went through the pregnancy by yourself?''

She nodded, but she didn't meet his gaze. Not quite the truth, he guessed, but she closed her eyes.

''I'm too tired to talk anymore.''

''Okay. We'll try again at lunchtime.''

She didn't answer. He picked up the tray, but he stared down at her for a moment. The food was helping her. She was going to regain her strength quickly.

But the mystery wasn't solved. And he intended to solve it before he let Isabella and Angel go away.

HE HANDLED Angel's ten-o'clock feeding as usual, except that he talked to her and played with her for about half an hour before he let her go back to sleep.

"Like mother, like daughter, little Angel. I can't keep either one of you awake." With a grin, he tucked the baby into her carrier. Then he took a quick look out the window. The wind seemed to be abating a little. He decided he'd better straighten up the living room before his mother arrived. And Tori and Jon. In fact, there might be a crowd before supper.

He wished he knew who Isabella was planning on visiting. No one he knew had mentioned relatives in New York. Nor had they had any visits from relatives from there. Was she all alone in New York? He didn't think so. The way she'd avoided his gaze when she said she'd had the baby alone made him think someone was around. And she was running from whoever that was.

He checked on Isabella. She was still sleeping, her face almost as innocent and young as Angel's.

He fixed himself a sandwich and turned on the television. He had a satellite dish and got the latest in weather. His family had been right. The snow was supposed to taper off this afternoon. Come to think of it, he didn't hear any wind now. He stepped to the window and opened the drapes.

It was a winter wonderland. There was the occasional little gust that stirred up snow crystals, but most of the snow had settled on the ground. He crossed to his front door, which looked down on Main Street, and saw several individuals outside, clearing off the sidewalks. He waved and went back inside.

Then he heard steps on the outside stairs. He opened the door just as Jon and Tori reached it.

"May we come in?" Tori asked, not waiting for an answer. She ducked under his arm and darted into the warmth.

"Hi, Jon." Russ said. "I hope you didn't have any trouble getting here. I think we're doing all right."

"No, no trouble. Except I tried to leave Tori at home with the baby. But Rosa will take care of him." Rosa was their housekeeper.

"Oh, Jon, come look. She's beautiful. Look at those curls!" Tori exclaimed.

Jon joined his wife at Angel's carrier. "Is she all right? Do I need to check her?"

"I don't think so. I think she's about a month old and she's eating every four hours. She has incredibly healthy lungs," Russ said.

"I know. So does Jonny. If anything, they get louder. Jonny is almost nine months old," Tori informed him. "I thought you might not know since you've avoided all the babies."

"I know."

Jon changed the subject. "Where's her mother?"

"In my bed."

Tori gasped.

Russ turned bright red. "I slept out here! On my air mattress, Tori. That's the only bed I had available."

"Oh. Of course. I'd break it to your mother in a

different way, Russ. She'll have you married before you know it."

"Tori, behave yourself," Jon ordered. "That's none of our business."

Russ said nothing.

"I'm serious, Jon! Janie wants Russ to remarry. She'll use any excuse she can find!"

For a minute Russ didn't even object. That meant he could keep Angel with him if he married Isabella. But marrying Isabella, even for Angel's sake, was a lot more complicated. She was a warm, passionate woman. He had withdrawn from life. They couldn't possibly live together unless one of them changed. And he couldn't change, so he returned to sanity. "Don't be ridiculous!"

Chapter Four

Isabella struggled up from a deep sleep to find three people staring at her. One she recognized.

"What?" she asked.

"Isabella, this is my cousin Tori and her husband, Dr. Jon Wilson. He'd like to examine you and ask a few questions. Tori thought you might feel more comfortable if she accompanied him."

"What kind of doctor?" she demanded. She noticed her voice was a little stronger, which encouraged her.

"A general practitioner," the doctor said. "I understand you've been running a fever."

"Yes...I think so, but according to him, I've been here three days. I don't remember them."

"What's the last thing you remember?" Jon asked as he moved to the bed and opened his black bag. Isabella let him check her temperature and pulse before she answered him. "I remember being in a hotel room in...in Chicago, I think."

"You don't remember driving to where Russ

found you?'' Tori asked, horror in her voice. ''It's a wonder you didn't have an accident.''

''But her instincts were good,'' Russ reminded his cousin. ''She kept herself and Angel safe until I came along to save them.''

''Probably the fever you had helped keep your baby warm.''

''Am I running a fever now?''

''A very slight one. I think an antibiotic would be a good thing just in case. Russ said he fed you breakfast this morning. Any difficulty keeping it down?''

''No.''

''Okay, I've got some samples here so Russ won't have to dig his way clear to the drugstore. Why don't we see if that will get you back on your feet again? Is that okay with you?''

She nodded.

''Not a big talker, are you?''

She shook her head. ''Thank you.''

''She has good manners,'' Russ muttered.

A knock sounded on the front door. Isabella glanced at Russ, seeing a worried look on his face. The other two seemed amused.

When Russ didn't move, Tori said, ''I think you have more company, Russ. Want me to open the door?''

''No, I'll get it.''

In no time he returned to the bedroom with two women. ''Isabella, this is my mother, Janie Randall, and my aunt, Anna Randall. She's a nurse.''

Isabella nodded to the two women, but she didn't say anything.

Janie sat on the side of the bed and patted Isabella's arm as if they were old friends. "Who are you visiting in Rawhide, dear? Maybe we know her."

"She doesn't live in town, so probably not," Isabella said quickly. She wasn't sure her great-aunt would keep her arrival a secret, and secrecy was essential. She knew that once she explained everything to her great-aunt, she would. But she wasn't sure she'd get the chance before her father called.

"None of us live in town, but we're a tight-knit community," Anna said.

"My aunt is elderly. I don't want anyone to surprise her."

Anna's eyes grew large, worrying Isabella. "Don't tell me you're Maria Paloni's great-niece? Of course, I should have remembered." Anna turned to Janie. "Remember, Janie? I told you about her wanting to talk to her great-niece that last time."

"She wanted to talk to me?"

"Yes," Anna said, turning to face Isabella, "but—" She stopped abruptly. "I'm sorry to have to tell you, Isabella. Maria died two weeks ago."

RUSS HADN'T REALIZED Maria Paloni had died. She was a charming old lady who'd lived near Rawhide for almost sixty years. She'd participated in community events for as long as he could remember.

Taken food to those in need. Offered to take care of children in times of stress.

Lately she hadn't been well, and his mother and the other Randall women had taken her food. Maybe that was why Isabella had heard the Randall name.

He convinced his mother and Anna to leave Isabella to mourn. She'd certainly looked stricken at the news. As they were leaving, pointing out the prepared food they'd left in his kitchen, Anna whispered that Nick was handling her estate.

"Okay. I'll check with him this afternoon."

"You'll be all right taking care of the baby?" Janie asked.

"I'll be fine. Angel is an easy baby."

"That's what people always say. If you get in trouble, call."

"Right, Mom."

Jon and Tori moved to leave, too. "Isabella seems to be getting well quickly, but make sure she takes all the antibiotics. Her fever should be completely gone in a couple of days," Jon said.

"Thanks for coming. I'll make sure she does."

"I can come stay with her if you need to go out," Tori said.

"How? Aren't you coming in to work this week?"

"Oh, yeah," Tori said with a grin. "I'll be in in the morning. Shall I stop by and say hi?"

"Up to you. I can't guarantee she'll be glad to see anyone."

"Okay. See you then."

Obviously he hadn't convinced Tori to stay away.

Russ walked back to check on Isabella. She'd fallen asleep. She still had a couple of tears on her pale cheeks. He moved closer and gently wiped them away with his thumb.

He decided he'd better call Nick right away. Nick was a cousin who hadn't known he was a Randall until last summer. He was, in fact, Gabe Randall's twin. But they'd separated at birth and Nick had been adopted. Now the two were reunited. And Nick was a lawyer.

As the only lawyer in Rawhide, he handled everything.

"Nick? It's Russ. Are you handling Mrs. Paloni's estate?"

"Well, I'm trying. I sent a letter to her beneficiary asking her to contact me, but I haven't heard from her."

"Is the beneficiary named Isabella? Um, I think she said her last name was Walker?"

"No, it's Isabella Paloni."

"Ah. I think she married and her aunt didn't know."

"Great-aunt. Are you sure we have the right woman?"

"I don't know. I found her on the road during the blizzard. She was sick and I brought her back to my place.

"I didn't find out Maria Paloni was the person

she came to visit until today. And I didn't know Mrs. Paloni had died."

"Hmm. Maybe I should come talk to her. Or she can come here if she wants."

"I don't think she's strong enough for that, Nick, even if it is only across the street. She's doing good to get to the bathroom on her own."

"Sounds bad. I'll be glad to come there. Is now all right? I've been worried about this."

"Sure. I'll get her sitting up so maybe you can talk."

He hung up the phone and realized that the sound in the background was the shower. She was taking a shower?

He hurried into the bedroom to confirm his realization. The bed was empty and her suitcase was open. He waited until the water stopped. "Isabella?"

"Yes?"

"Nick is coming over to see you."

"Who's Nick?"

"He's handling your great-aunt's estate."

"Let me guess. He's another member of your huge family."

Russ chuckled softly. He recognized the irritation in her voice. "I'm afraid so. Are you ready for some new pajamas? I've got some clean ones."

"I'm getting dressed."

"Are you sure you're up to it?" he asked, concern filling him.

''Yes. I feel much stronger after eating breakfast.''

''All right. Come out when you're ready.''

His mother had left one of Red's famous chocolate cakes on the kitchen counter. He thought that might give Isabella some energy. And he knew Nick loved Red's cakes. Besides, he wanted a piece, too.

When Nick got there, he found Russ happily chowing down on a huge piece of chocolate cake. ''Is that Red's chocolate cake?''

''Yep. And your piece is right there.''

Nick picked it up with a grin and settled on the sofa. He'd just taken a big bite when he looked down and saw Angel asleep in the carrier.

''What the hell?'' he managed.

''DON'T HURT MY BABY!'' Isabella shrieked from the door to the bedroom. She rushed forward, but Russ was already holding Angel.

''Hey! I wouldn't hurt a baby. But no one told me there was a baby,'' the stranger said, glaring at Russ.

''Sorry, Nick. I didn't think it would be such a surprise.'' Russ turned to Isabella. He opened his mouth to speak. Then he closed it again, his gaze going from her head to her toes. She'd put on a navy pantsuit with a striped knit top under the jacket and navy shoes. She wore makeup and had forced her wayward curls into a French knot, all sleek and sophisticated.

"Wow. That's a big change, Isabella."

She stiffened. "I don't do lawyer interviews in my pajamas." She held out her arms for her baby.

"Look, she's still asleep. Let's put her back in the carrier and put it in the bedroom. That way she won't wake up."

Reluctantly she nodded.

After he came back to the living room, he pointed out her cake and a glass of milk. "Thought you might need a little energy."

Surprisingly, she felt hungry for the cake. Maybe because it was chocolate. "Did you make it?" she asked the stranger.

"No, Red did."

"Another member of your family?" she asked as she looked at Russ.

"Sort of. Now, do you want me to go in the bedroom and leave you alone with Nick?"

She cast Nick a look. He was an attractive man, but she didn't feel as confident of him as she did Russ. "No, you can stay."

Russ and Nick exchanged a look, but Russ sat back down and continued eating his chocolate cake. When she took her first bite, she understood his enthusiasm.

"Do you mind if I record our meeting?" Nick asked, putting a small tape recorder on the coffee table.

"No. That will be fine."

Nick picked up the tape recorder, announcing into it the date and time and the participants. Then he looked at Isabella. "Are you Isabella Paloni, great-niece of Maria Paloni, deceased resident of Rawhide?"

"Yes, I am. I got married about eleven months ago, but after my husband's death, I took back my maiden name."

"Were you aware that you are the beneficiary to Mrs. Paloni's estate?"

"She wrote me that she was leaving me everything."

"Is that why you came here?"

"No! I came because I didn't even know she existed. When I received her letter, I called her. She invited me to come."

Isabella's eyes filled with tears.

"Have a drink of milk," Russ said softly, leaning toward her. When she did so, he said, "Good girl. Now eat some more cake."

Nick turned off the tape recorder. "Want to wait a few minutes?"

"Please."

"How old is your baby?" Nick asked. To her surprise, he looked interested.

"She's six weeks."

"Her father passed away before she was born?"

"Yes," she said, glancing at Russ.

"My wife is expecting in seven and a half months. We just found out at Thanksgiving."

Russ looked surprised. "I didn't know. Congratulations, Nick."

"Thanks. I don't exactly know what to expect. I've never been around babies."

"You'll learn quickly," Isabella said, relaxing a little.

"Well, my twin and his wife, my wife's sister, just had twin babies about a month ago, so I'm learning a little."

"Twins?" she asked in horror. "I don't know how anyone manages. I got punch-drunk waking up every four hours with Angel."

"That's her name?" Nick asked.

"Actually, her name is Angela, but I call her Angel most of the time."

"Ready to start again?" Nick asked. "Maybe after we finish I can see Angel. I'd like to bring my wife over to see her, too."

"I think Mom and Anna brought enough food for dinner tonight," Russ said. "Why don't the two of you join us?"

"That would be great," Nick replied. "Sarah is tired of my company after the blizzard. Is that okay with you, Isabella?"

"Yes, of course." She didn't feel she had a choice. It wasn't her house.

Nick turned the tape recorder on again. "Now, Miss Paloni, are you aware of the extent of your great-aunt's estate?"

"No. It doesn't matter."

Nick looked surprised. "But—"

"She offered me something more important to me than money. She offered me a home, family.

But it was too late.'' Again her eyes filled with tears. Her teeth settled in her bottom lip, trying to prevent a major meltdown.

Russ leaned forward. ''You don't have any family?''

She kept her head bent, not wanting to face him. ''I do, but I don't want anything to do with them.''

''Why?'' Russ demanded.

''I really don't see the need to talk about this. I was going to live with my great-aunt, me and Angel, but now we can't.''

Nick intervened in what had become a very personal conversation. ''But you can live in her house, because it's yours now.''

She hadn't thought of that. But even if she lived there, she wouldn't have what she wanted for Angel. ''I was hoping to have a family for Angel.''

Nick said calmly, ''You might marry and provide Angel with brothers and sisters.''

''No!'' She didn't bother to explain, but her answer was firm. Very firm.

Both men stared at her. She clarified. ''I never intend to marry again. I won't give some man control over me or my daughter.''

After a moment of silence, Nick said, ''I gather your marriage was not a happy one. Um, how did your husband die?''

She looked him in the eye. ''I didn't kill him. I consider my father to be the killer, though my husband died in a car accident.'' Dark thoughts filled her as she added, ''But it was my father's fault.''

"Finish your cake and milk, honey. You're going to wear yourself out with all this emotion." Russ watched her to make sure she did what he'd said.

"Fine. You're always urging me to eat." She took a bite of cake. "It's very good cake."

"Red is famous for it."

"You didn't say who Red is," she reminded him.

"He's my grandmother."

Nick protested even more than Isabella. "You're just confusing her. That's not fair."

"No, it's not," Isabella said, relaxing against the sofa.

"Why not? It got you to smile, didn't it?" Russ asked.

"Yes, it did, but now give me the real answer."

"Okay. When my dad and his brothers were little, their mom died giving birth to my youngest uncle, Chad. Red was a crippled cowboy who did odd jobs for our grandfather. He asked him to move into the house and help him raise the boys. My grandfather died, but Red stayed on and took care of the house. Then Uncle Jake, the oldest brother, realized that if his brothers didn't marry, they'd have no kids to leave the ranch to."

Isabella frowned. "Wait a minute. Why did you say if the others didn't marry? What was wrong with Jake?"

"He was divorced and thought marriage wasn't for him," Russ said with a grin. "But once he managed to marry the other three off, his new sisters-in-law decided he deserved the same treatment."

"Smart ladies," Isabella said.

"You met two of them today. Janie and Anna."

Her eyebrows went up and she nodded.

"That's how matchmaking became a tradition in the Randall family. We're known for it throughout the county."

"They don't get crazy about it," Nick put in. "But if they can give a match a nudge, they help it along."

"Did they bring about your marriage?" she asked Nick.

"I didn't need any help. Once I got out of the big city, Denver, that is, I could tell the glitter from the real gold. When you meet Sarah, you'll realize how perfect she is."

Russ smiled. "He's not prejudiced at all."

"Of course not."

"You weren't prejudiced about Abby, either, were you?" Nick said. Then he immediately apologized. "Sorry, Russ."

Isabella looked from one to the other, but both men were silent. "What? What happened?"

Russ cleared his throat. "My wife, pregnant with our child, died about eighteen months ago. Most people don't mention her."

"But don't you want them to?" Isabella asked in surprise.

"What do you mean?" Russ asked harshly.

"If you don't talk about a person, your memories fade. Don't you want to remember Abby?"

NICK LEFT SHORTLY after Isabella's remark. Russ wasn't surprised. He was stunned by her words and couldn't carry on conversation anymore. And Nick was upset that he'd upset Russ. And since Isabella wasn't interested in talking about Maria Paloni's estate, he said they'd discuss it later.

Russ had opened the window curtain in the living room and was staring out at the snow-swept land. Suddenly he remembered a time when he and Abby had joined her students sledding on the school grounds. She'd laughed and chased after the children as if she were a child herself. He could suddenly see her so clearly. And the time he'd watched her teach school. She'd been so gentle, so tender with the little children.

They'd shared their first Christmas together, engaged. It had been special because Abby made it that way. She loved his family and jumped into the preparations for Christmas with great enthusiasm. She had no family of her own. None at all. Sometimes he worried that maybe she loved his family more than she loved him.

But Abby seemed to understand him better than anyone in the world. And she always let him know how important he was to her. Him and their child. She was so happy to have his child. She hadn't felt exactly well. But she never complained.

Every day had been a miracle with Abby.

Then suddenly she wasn't there anymore, taken by an aneurysm in the early stages of her pregnancy. He'd gone up into the mountains because he couldn't face the loss. If Tori and Jon hadn't come to find him, he would've died up there.

Then he'd tried to live without really living. He knew now that had been wrong. Abby wouldn't have wanted it. He'd almost killed his memories of Abby, too. Until Isabella's remark today.

The door to his bedroom opened, and Isabella, who'd gone to bed after Nick's visit, came out. "Do you need any help getting things ready?"

"No, I want you to sit down. Angel will be up in a few minutes. I'll fix the bottle, but you can feed her."

"Thank you, Russ."

"Did you get some rest?"

"Yes, I did, but I'm feeling better. Just…sad about great-aunt Maria."

"You'd never met her?"

"No. My father kept her a secret." She studied her hands linked together in her lap. "He tried to control everything. It's a wonder I ever got the letter. But she said in the letter she'd sent it as simply as possible, so he wouldn't notice. If she'd sent it from her lawyer, he would've opened it."

"That's against the law."

Isabella shrugged.

"Why did you get married?"

"I thought Timothy was different. And I thought he would fight my father. But he was too weak."

"So you were coming here so your aunt could help you fight your father?"

"I thought we could be a family, the three of us. That was what I wanted."

"Why not remarry and have more children?"

"Because I don't trust men."

"So Angel's never going to have a father?"

Isabella lifted her chin. "I'll take care of her. She won't need a father."

"Yes, she will. Every little girl needs a mother and a father." He paced a few steps, then turned to look at her. "I want Angel to have everything. She's such a sweet baby."

Isabella's face softened. "She's wonderful, isn't she?"

"Yeah."

"But I'm not marrying again."

He stared at her for several minutes. Should he suggest it? Because he knew already he was going to need some kind of defense against his mother and father's efforts.

"I know how Angel can have a daddy and plenty of family. Without you giving up any control."

She stared at him. "How?" she asked slowly.

"Marry me."

Chapter Five

She stared at him. Then she gave him her answer. "No!"

"Wait! Let me explain. I don't want to marry, either."

"Well, you're sure going about it the wrong way. Someone might accept if you go around asking."

"But I want to marry you for that very reason," he continued as if she hadn't spoken.

"That doesn't make sense."

"Yes, it does, if you'll let me explain."

She nodded, watching him closely, as if he was an unpredictable creature.

"You know my...my wife died summer a year ago. I stopped living. I existed. I closed myself off to every emotion. I hid behind the numbers I work with. I avoided all weddings, babies, parties, celebrations. I was cowardly, I know. When you and Angel came into my life, you forced me back to life. I fell in love again."

She looked alarmed and he hurriedly added,

"Don't panic. And don't take offense. I fell in love with Angel."

Her face softened. As it always did when her daughter was involved. He loved that about her. Liked. Liked that, that was what he meant.

"What I want is to be Angel's father. What you want for Angel is family. I've got more family than anyone you know."

"I'll agree with you there," she said, relaxing enough to smile at him.

"Don't you see? Neither of us wants a marital relationship. But if we marry, no one will try to marry us off. I'll sign whatever restrictions you want."

"I have to warn you, Russ. My father will probably try to take away any money I have. I'll have to get a job to help support the two of us."

"That's the beauty of our plan. Not only do I have family, I also have money. I've made more than a good living. And Tori does my investments. She's a genius."

"Tori? The doctor's wife?"

"Yeah. Amazing, isn't it?"

"But you shouldn't have to support the two of us." She wouldn't look at him. "That wouldn't be fair. Besides..." She hesitated, as if she had something else to confess.

"What is it, honey?" Russ asked softly, stepping over to sit beside her on the sofa.

"My father can be very unpleasant."

Russ kept waiting, expecting something more. Finally he said, "That's it? He can be unpleasant?"

"Okay, he can be a bastard. Especially if he has power over you."

"But he has no power over me."

"He'll try to ruin you."

"And you think I would walk away and leave Angel to him?"

"My husband did. Well, he didn't walk away. He decided to give in, thinking it would make him rich. Daddy bought him a fast car. It killed him."

"Your husband gave you up for a sports car?" Russ asked, astounded. Now he understood Isabella's attitude toward marriage...and men. "You'll be safe with me, honey. If I want a sports car, I can buy one myself."

"Russ, I don't think you've thought about this enough. I think you're acting on impulse."

"Just think about it. Now that the storm has stopped and you're getting better, you're going to have to make some decisions. Oh, by the way, Nick sent a letter to you in New York. Will your father get it?"

She shuddered. "Yes. That means he'll call Nick and probably show up here. When did he send the letter?"

"We'll ask him tonight. Just think about what I've said. We'll talk again later." He finished just as a knock came on the front door and Angel let out a roar.

"She never starts off easy, does she," Russ said

as he picked her up. ''Why don't you change her while I get the door and make the bottle.'' He reluctantly handed the baby to Isabella.

He opened the door and invited Nick and Sarah in.

''I hope we didn't wake the baby,'' Sarah said, her gaze searching the room for the source of the noise.

Russ grinned. ''Nah. She's right on schedule. Isabella, this is Sarah, the sweeter half of the McMillans.''

''Hello,'' Isabella said as she changed her daughter. ''But isn't your name Randall? I thought Russ said—''

''I was adopted at birth and that's my adopted parents' name. I haven't changed it.''

''You might as well,'' Sarah said with a smile. ''Everyone calls us Randalls,'' she added for Isabella's benefit.

''As soon as Russ gets the bottle ready, we'll be able to talk. Angel is rather single-minded at this stage,'' Isabella said with a smile.

''May I hold her?'' Sarah asked, sitting on the sofa beside Isabella while Russ went into the kitchen to fix the baby's bottle. ''We're expecting a baby in early summer and we're so excited.''

Isabella transferred her tiny daughter to Sarah's arms. ''I do apologize for her behavior.''

''This will take care of it,'' Russ assured them as he presented the bottle to Sarah. ''Put this in her mouth to give us some relief.''

“Me? I can feed her?” Sarah asked. “I have fed the twins, of course. It takes two to handle feeding at my sister’s.”

“I can’t imagine taking care of twins,” Isabella said with a shudder. “It shouldn’t be so hard to handle one baby, but it’s the fact that there’s no letup. Every four hours, no matter what, she demands your attention.”

They all laughed as Sarah gave Angel her bottle. Angel immediately began to suck. “Well, she’s certainly enthusiastic. You don’t have to worry about her appetite.”

“No,” Isabella agreed.

Russ moved toward the kitchen again. “I’ll get dinner ready so we can eat after Angel finishes,” he said, excusing himself.

Nick followed him to the kitchen. “Maybe I can help.”

“Sure.” In about two minutes they’d transferred the food from the oven to the table. “We still have cake for dessert,” Russ added.

“Terrific. Uh, listen, I have something to tell Isabella that…well, I’m afraid it may upset her.”

“What is it?” Russ asked.

“I can’t tell you. You’re not my client.”

“Nick?” Sarah called. “Come look at her. Isn’t she beautiful?”

Nick left Russ in the kitchen and went out to admire the baby.

Russ followed. “She gets her curls from her mother,” he said.

Sarah looked at Isabella. ‘‘Your hair is naturally curly, too?’’

‘‘I’m afraid so.’’

‘‘Oh, you’re lucky. My hair doesn’t do anything!’’

‘‘And I love it straight,’’ Nick said with a grin. ‘‘It’s just like you—perfect.’’

Sarah rolled her eyes and laughed.

‘‘Is Angel through eating?’’ Russ asked. ‘‘I’ve got dinner on the table.’’

‘‘Yes, of course. I’ll just put her down in the bedroom,’’ Isabella said, standing and reaching for the baby. Sarah gave her up reluctantly. She turned to Russ. ‘‘She is so sweet. The boys are fun, too, but not as sweet as a little girl.’’

‘‘Hmm, sounds to me like a little prejudice,’’ Nick protested.

Russ ignored the teasing. ‘‘When are you going to tell her?’’

‘‘What?’’ Sarah asked, confused.

‘‘I’ll wait until after we eat. I don’t want to spoil her meal.’’ Nick quickly explained to Sarah what he was talking about.

‘‘I knew there was something wrong. You become very noncommittal when there’s something wrong,’’ Sarah said.

‘‘With good reason,’’ Nick muttered as Isabella came back into the room.

They moved to the table and settled down with chicken spaghetti and steamed broccoli for their meal, along with garlic bread.

"This is delicious," Isabella said. "I would love to have the recipe."

"It's B.J.'s, but I'm sure she'll share it," Sarah said.

"Who is B.J.?"

Russ grinned. "Another family member. She married Jake, the oldest Randall. She's Toby, Caroline and Josh's mother."

"And a very good vet," Nick added.

"And she takes time to make meals like this?" Isabella asked. "She must move nonstop."

"Nah. Caroline's in medical school in Chicago, Josh is away at university, and Toby's married and has a baby. She only works part-time, mostly on their own stock."

"Well, her life's a snap," Isabella drawled.

Sarah laughed. "It's not easy being a member of the Randalls. I gave it considerable thought before I agreed."

Nick's head whipped up. "Hey! It didn't take you that long!"

"Of course not, dear. I was only teasing."

Conversation flowed back and forth as they ate, and Russ couldn't help thinking Isabella fit in well. But he was anxious to hear about the new problem.

He told Isabella and Sarah to remain seated while he and Nick cleared the table and served the rest of Red's cake.

"Oh, I shouldn't have any, but I don't think I can resist," Sarah said, longing in her voice.

"I think you should have some cake. A balanced

diet includes some treats, you know. It will make your baby happier,'' Isabella said with a smile.

''Ooh, I like your way of thinking. I'll have to remember that when I go in to see Jon in a couple of weeks.''

''Jon is your doctor?''

''Jon is the only doctor,'' Nick said, smiling, ''but we'd choose him, anyway.''

''Does he treat his own family? I thought doctors weren't supposed to do that.''

''Doc came out of retirement to deliver Tori's baby, but Jon was right there, of course. Otherwise, he hasn't had a conflict. Besides, he's related to half the town now. That would make things difficult.''

''And Caroline is planning on returning to Rawhide to practice when she finishes,'' Russ added.

''When will that be?'' Isabella asked.

''I'm not sure,'' Russ said. ''I think she's going to specialize in pediatrics, so she may have two years left.''

He and Nick brought the cake to the table and rejoined the women. Silence fell as they all took blissful bites of the cake.

Then Nick said, ''Uh, Isabella, I need to talk to you about a phone call I received today. I can wait for privacy, but it needs to be tonight.''

She put down her fork and looked at him. ''My father got my letter and called you.''

''Yes, he did.''

Sarah offered to move away from the table if Isabella wanted privacy.

"No. Everyone will know about my father soon enough. What did he say?"

"He said you showed him the letter and asked him to handle everything. He suggested I box up your aunt's belongings and send them directly to him. Don't even bother going through them."

Everyone watched Isabella for her reaction.

"What did Great-aunt Maria have that he wants?"

"Smart lady," Nick said.

"What did you tell him?" Isabella asked without waiting for an answer.

"I said, I see, and thanks for calling."

"Nice, but that certainly didn't satisfy him, did it?"

"No. But I told him we were in the early stages."

"And?"

"He ordered me to ship everything, again emphasizing no need to go through it."

"Again I ask you what Aunt Maria had that he wants?"

Russ looked at Isabella. She was quite different from Abby. His wife had been quiet, rather shy, gentle. Isabella was determined, strong.

Nick hadn't answered. Now he asked a question. "What is Paloni Industries?"

Isabella didn't answer right away. Finally she said, "It's the family company. It's been around for 150 years, and my father has been in charge for the last thirty years. He's expanded it a lot."

''Your great-aunt owned controlling interest.''

Isabella froze. ''That's impossible!''

''No. According to what I can determine, your aunt gave your father power of attorney some time ago. She has received huge sums of money from its operations. One year the money stopped coming and she threatened to reclaim her power of attorney. There was a check sent to her almost immediately. She was going to have the company audited.''

''Good for her,'' Isabella said, determination in her eyes.

Nick watched her carefully. ''So now you own controlling interest in Paloni Industries. And unless you execute a power of attorney, you control everything.''

She clearly hadn't thought through the significance of Nick's words until he explained it. She processed the words, but they still didn't make sense. Then she laughed. A mere bubble at first. Then a chuckle. Then her laughter became almost hysterical.

''Isabella?'' Russ said. ''Are you all right?''

She tried to pull her laughter under control, but it wasn't easy. ''You don't understand. My father has no use for women. He believes all the power belongs to the man. And if he wants to give things to his woman, that's acceptable. But if he doesn't think she deserves nice things, she doesn't get them.''

Nick muttered, ''A Neanderthal.''

''Exactly. And to think that he had to rely on my

aunt's goodness to maintain the position that he let everyone believe was his by right. And now he has to rely on me.'' She looked at Nick. ''He's planning on hiding that fact. He's planning on taking over the company and giving me nothing.''

''Probably,'' Nick agreed. ''Of course he won't be able to.''

''Why not?''

''The first time he tries, we'll file suit against him, remove him from his position as president and chairman.''

''I can do that?''

''You can do it tomorrow if you want. As of now, you have controlling interest. Your father must be in hell.''

''Good.'' Her face hardened and there was none of the sweetness and gentleness Russ had seen when she held her child.

''Is that what you want me to do?''

''Not yet. I want him to suffer awhile.''

Sarah gasped. Then she covered her mouth with her hand. ''I'm sorry. But don't you love your father?''

''No. I loved him when I was an innocent child. I was his only child, and he spoiled me. Not only with toys, things, but with his time, his affection. But he remarried after my mother's death and he had another child. A boy. Suddenly I didn't exist. Only his son. The boy has been ruined. He's weak and lazy.

''My father can't see that, of course. Which will

eventually be his downfall. But I felt like the proverbial child outside the candy store, unable to share in anything.''

''I'm so sorry,'' Sarah said. ''I understand your anger. But...'' She looked at her husband, then went on, ''I've always heard that anger hurts the person who is angry more than it hurts the person the anger is directed at.''

''Maybe because a person is angry because they are powerless, as I was. No longer. Now I have the power.''

Then she looked at Russ. ''Do you remember the question you asked me to think about?''

''Yes,'' he said quietly, wondering where the conversation was going.

''My answer is yes.''

''All right.''

''You're sure? I want to be sure Angel is protected, no matter what happens to me.''

''Surely you don't think your father would harm you in any way?'' Nick asked, frowning.

''My father would kill his own sainted mother if it meant he could keep his wealth and power. That's why I must have a will in place first thing in the morning. And I want a list of all the Randalls as possible legal guardians, but my father, or anyone blood-related to him, cannot be considered.''

''As soon as your father realizes you're here and I won't fall for his lies, he'll come here, you realize,'' Nick said.

''Right. How soon can we marry, Russ?''

''Three days,'' Russ said slowly.

''Don't take his calls for three days. Can you do that?''

Nick gave a small smile. ''I've stalled before, Isabella.''

''So he won't know the Randall name at all, because you use your legal name. That's perfect.''

''I'm glad to please.''

''We'll draw up papers that give Russ control of the shares if anything happens to me, holding them in trust for Angel. And that control will transfer to whomever takes over as legal guardian if something happens to him. Don't worry, Russ. You'll be compensated for your efforts.''

''Buying me, Isabella? Like your father bought your husband?''

''No! But it's only fair. Don't you see?''

''No, I'm afraid I don't. If something happens to you, everyone will say I married you for your money. So, unfortunately, I must decline the honor of being your husband.''

''What? But you asked me!''

Nick and Sarah were silently watching the argument, trying to hide their surprise.

''I'm sorry, Isabella. I can't marry you.''

Chapter Six

After a moment of stunned silence, Isabella pushed back her chair. Before she left the table, she looked at Nick. ''Can you give me a ride to my aunt's house?''

''Of course, but it would be better if you let me have someone clean it before you see it.''

''No, thank you. If you can drop us off tonight, that will do.''

''Us?'' Russ questioned.

She turned her big blue eyes on him, but her expression was cold. ''I wouldn't think of leaving without my baby.''

''Leaving? I thought you were going to go look at your aunt's house. You can't stay there.''

''Why not? According to my attorney, I own it.'' She left the room.

''Nick, you've got to stop her. She's still weak. She needs help with the baby,'' Russ said.

Sarah looked at him. ''You expect her to let you help with anything after you reject her in front of us? You're out of your mind.'' She turned her gaze to Nick. ''Dear, why don't we take her and Angel to our place? Tomorrow the two of you can go look at Mrs. Paloni's house while the baby sleeps.''

''You go talk to her while I deal with Mr. Smooth here,'' Nick said as he gestured to Russ.

''Hey!'' Russ protested as Sarah followed Isabella. ''I didn't do anything wrong.''

Nick shook his head. ''You ask a woman to marry you and then when she accepts you say, sorry, I changed my mind? And you think you did nothing wrong. Even I know that much about women.''

''But if I marry her now, people will think I'm marrying her for her money. When I offered marriage, it was because we each would get something from the marriage.''

''Other than the normal stuff, you mean?''

''No! There was no normal stuff. I want to be a father to Angel, and she wants a family for Angel. That was it.''

''So what's changed? Not that I approve of your kind of marriage, but if that was okay before, what's made it bad now?''

''She's filthy rich and wants to pay me to take care of Angel. I offered to take care of both of them, but no one will believe that!''

Suddenly Isabella was standing behind him. ''Oh, so it's your pride that's hurt.''

''Yes, my pride is hurt.''

''I knew I couldn't trust men!'' she muttered.

"What do you mean? Of course you can trust me!" Russ roared, unusual behavior for him.

"Can I? I need you to promise to take care of Angel if something happens to me, because I have no one else. And you reject me because of your pride."

Russ stood and looked at her. He hadn't realized... It had never occurred to him how his decision would affect both Isabella and Angel.

After gazing into her blue eyes, he reached out and pulled her into his embrace. "I apologize, Isabella. Of course, we'll marry. But you have to do something else with the money."

"But it's all I have to give you."

"No. You will have already given me Angel. I'm going to be Angel's daddy. That's the greatest gift of all." Suddenly, holding her in his arms felt too intimate. He backed away. "Okay?"

"Can we do that, Nick?" Isabella asked.

"Sure. We can put Tori in charge of everything financial for Angel. She's a genius with money."

"That's what Russ says. Will she mind?"

"I don't think so, but we'll check with her first thing in the morning." He paused and looked at his wife over Isabella's shoulder. Then his gaze came back to the couple in front of him. "So you two are really going to marry in three days?"

Russ and Isabella looked at each other. Then Russ nodded. "Yes, we are."

"A marriage of convenience?" Nick asked.

Russ stopped him. "That's between the two of

us. It's a real marriage in terms of legality. And I'm sure we'll decide to give the appearance of a real marriage, because it is forever, right, Isabella?"

"Of course."

Nick looked at both of them, as if he had a question, but then he simply nodded. "You'd better put the family on notice, then. There's a lot to get done."

"I can take care of the baby while you go to Buffalo tomorrow to get your license. You could even have lunch out together to celebrate your engagement," Sarah offered.

"That's so nice of you, Sarah, but surely it won't take that long," Isabella said.

"Yes, it will," Russ assured her. "Buffalo is an hour away, so it will take two or three hours. We might as well add lunch. I bet you haven't had a lunch without Angel since she was born, anyway."

"No, but...she might miss me."

"And we'll both miss her. It will be good for everyone. Thanks, Sarah."

RUSS WAITED until both Isabella and Angel were asleep that night before he called the ranch. Angel would be up an hour later, but he'd be finished with his phone call by then. He hoped.

"Mom?" he said when Janie came to the phone.

"Russ? Is everything all right?"

"Yeah. But I have some news for you. Are you sitting down?"

"No. Should I sit down?"

''It might be a good idea.'' He heard a murmur of voices.

''Are the others there with you?''

''Yes, we were discussing...things.''

''Well, here's something else for you to discuss. You're getting a new grandbaby.''

Stunned silence.

He decided he shouldn't have announced his news in that way. ''No, I haven't gotten someone pregnant. But Isabella and I are getting married. I'm going to be Angel's daddy.''

His mother screamed and dropped the phone.

Then a male voice spoke. ''Son? What did you just tell your mother?''

''I told her Isabella and I are getting married. I'm going to be Angel's daddy.''

After a deep breath, Pete said, ''Congratulations. When do I get to meet these two additions to the family?''

''We'll come out tomorrow afternoon after we go to Buffalo to get the license. We're going to have lunch there, so it will probably be around two.''

''Just a minute,'' Pete said.

Russ heard him talking to the others, but he must have had his hand over the receiver because Russ couldn't make out the words.

''Your mother says for Isabella to bring her luggage. She and the baby shouldn't stay there with you. It will cause talk. Besides, they'll need to consult with Isabella to make sure the wedding is what she wants. What date are you planning on?"

Russ cleared his throat. "Uh, three days from now."

"Friday? Is there a reason for this rush?"

"Yeah, but it's not what you're thinking."

"Tell me."

"Isabella is afraid her father will try to harm her before we marry if he finds out about it."

"Harm her? Not just stop the wedding?"

"Yeah. Mrs. Paloni owned controlling interest in the family company. She gave Isabella's father controlling interest with a power of attorney. When she died, that became null and void unless Isabella does the same thing. They don't...uh, Isabella and her father aren't happy with each other."

"Son, if that's the only reason for the marriage, you know we'll protect her without you marrying her. Mrs. Paloni was a friend."

"I know, Dad. But I want to be Angel's father. Isabella doesn't intend to remarry in the traditional sense, but this works for both of us. You should see Angel, Dad. She's a sweetheart."

"I've heard Isabella isn't too bad, either."

Russ stiffened. "She's not like Abby. But it will work. It will just be different."

"Okay, son. We'll see the three of you tomorrow."

"Thanks, Dad. Good night."

His father had accepted his choice. His mom might not, but he had his dad's support. And if Mr.

Paloni showed up, his entire family would support him. And that wasn't small potatoes.

When Angel stirred at ten, Russ had the bottle ready, so the baby wouldn't wake her mother. Isabella had been exhausted, though she was recovering quickly.

Once Russ had the baby changed and the bottle in her mouth, he sat down in a chair and began a conversation with his soon-to-be daughter.

"Listen, Angel, I'm going to be your daddy in a few days. I want you to know that I will always love you, no matter what you do. I may not like what you do, I may even punish you, but I will always love you. And not just because you're pretty.

"Being pretty is nice, but being pretty inside is even better, and your mommy and I will make sure you're that. We'll make sure you learn the important lessons, and we'll keep you safe from anyone who wants to hurt you, especially your grandpa. I've got some better family for you. You'll love them.

"And so will your mommy. She's had a hard time of it, so I'm going to take care of her, too. Your real daddy is gone, so I'm going to replace him."

He burped his new daughter and then settled her in her carrier. "We're getting you a baby bed soon. Maybe tomorrow. You're going to stay with your new grandparents for a couple of days. And soon you'll meet your new cousin, my brother's baby. Everything will be fine."

He hoped Isabella took to the changes in her life as well as Angel would. She expected to be in control. But he didn't want her hurting his family's feelings.

And he didn't want them hurting her. She'd been hurt enough.

RUSS HAD OATMEAL ready for breakfast when Isabella awoke the next morning. "You're going to spoil me, Russ."

"I'm an early riser. It's not a problem."

"But I'll be expected to make it after we're married."

He looked at her, not sure what point she was making. "Well, I suppose we can work that out, but I have to get up early for work and I'll want to feed Angel, since I can't stay home, so I might as well make breakfast."

"You're not worried that people won't think you're macho if I don't make breakfast?"

Russ gave her a wry smile. "You remember me telling you about Red?"

"Yes."

"Well, he taught my father and my uncles that if they wanted to eat, they'd better learn to do household chores. And that's how we were raised. In addition, each of their wives had her own interests. Megan was an interior designer. Chad, her husband, once made a remark about her job being to buy a sofa, and he slept on a sofa for a while. B.J. is a vet, a darn good one. Anna is a nurse and a midwife. And my mom, well, she did the paperwork for her dad's ranch and is a good cowhand. None of them considers cooking or cleaning a career. It's a necessity for everybody."

"How liberated. Are...are you sure?"

"Oh, yeah. You'll see when you move in out there."

"What are you talking about?" she asked in sudden stern tones. "I'm going to live in Aunt Maria's house."

"If you were completely over your illness, I'd agree with you. But my parents think it looks bad for you to continue to live with me before our marriage. They're a little old-fashioned, I'll admit."

"It's not their decision," she returned firmly.

"You're right. But *if* you stay with them, you'll have help with Angel, your meals will be taken care of, and you'll have an opportunity to get to know the family you're getting for Angel."

"I can take care of both of us."

"Obviously, since you did after she was born. Until you got sick. I want you completely well for our wedding. And they can go over to Mrs. Paloni's house with you. Megan is good at decorating. And she can sell anything you don't want to keep."

"But there's no need, Russ. I can manage."

"I know you can, but when it's not necessary, why take the hard route?"

"They'll think I'm lazy. Taking advantage of you and them."

"I promise I won't think that, and they won't, either."

"They're too good to be true. In my family, if someone does something for you, they demand payment, and it's always more than you can afford."

"It will only be for three days. Will you try it just for me? If it's horrible, tell me, and I'll get you out of there."

Isabella finally nodded but he could see the worry and reluctance in her eyes.

WHEN THEY REACHED Buffalo, Russ was uneasy. Isabella had slept most of the way, and he'd been left to his memories of driving to Buffalo with Abby. She'd been snuggled up next to him, planning their future. Everything had been exactly as he wanted it. If it wasn't, she'd changed it so it was. She never argued with him.

Isabella saw things differently. He suspected she'd argue with him just to be sure she could. She'd finally agreed to stay at his parents' home for three days, unless she didn't like it. And he knew she wasn't joking.

"We're here, Isabella. Ready?"

She gave him a sleepy look that made him want to cuddle her against him. That thought startled him. No, if it was Angel, he'd cuddle her. Not Isabella.

Inside, he discovered she intended to keep her family name, Paloni.

"Are you sure?"

"Yes, I am," she said calmly. "Why wouldn't I?"

He didn't want to say what he thought of her father. Besides, it didn't matter. She'd be called Randall in Rawhide.

"When I adopt Angel, her name will change."

Her gaze riveted on him. "Oh, no. Her name will be the same as mine."

"Then you'd better plan on having my name, because she's going to be my daughter. That was part of our agreement."

Chapter Seven

"I don't remember your requiring the same name," Isabella whispered fiercely.

"Kids would ask her why she doesn't have the same name, and they would tease her. It would cause awkwardness with her teachers when I talked to them. It would make her feel that she doesn't belong. I'm not letting you do that to Angel." Russ stood there, his hands on his hips, glaring at her.

"Obviously you've done a lot of thinking about this!"

"Obviously you haven't."

Isabella turned and walked out the door of the office. With an apology to the woman waiting for them, Russ went after her.

"Where do you think you're going?"

She spun around. "Somewhere I can think!"

Russ had been ready to lay into her again, but the tears in her eyes undid him. "Okay. How about we go to lunch in a restaurant? I'll be quiet and give you some time."

His offer seemed to floor her. "We can do that?"

"Of course. I know the perfect place." He drove them to a small, intimate restaurant. Once they were seated at a table and their meals ordered, he excused himself to go talk to the owner, an old friend of the Randall family, leaving her alone.

When he saw the waitress bringing their food fifteen minutes later, he said goodbye to his friend and returned to the table. He slid into his chair and greeted her, but he didn't ask any questions.

After the waitress left, she asked, "Aren't you going to demand to know my decision?"

"No, I figure you'll tell me when you've decided."

She put her fork down and stared at him in exasperation. "Are you always like this?"

"Like what?"

"Reasonable!"

He laughed. "And that's a bad thing?"

"You know it isn't. I... Thank you for giving me time."

"You hadn't thought about the changes our marriage will make in your life. And you aren't even settled in Rawhide yet. That's a lot of change."

"Yes. And I would be making it more difficult by keeping my maiden name and doing the same to Angel. Of course we'll take your name."

"Good girl," he said with a warm smile. Her return smile was tentative, but at least it was a smile.

"When will you find out about adopting Angel?"

"I thought I'd pick up a form today, if they have one. No sense in delaying as long as we're in agreement. That puts both you and Angel under my protection."

"I don't want you to be hurt. My father can be...brutal if it suits his purposes."

"Quit worrying about me. My family will stand beside me. He'll be the outsider if he comes here. And if he doesn't come here, he won't be a bother."

"I hope not."

"What do you think he can do?"

"He'll get his lawyers to trick us, or harass us, or..."

"And you're thinking Nick is just a country attorney who won't know what to do?"

"There is a difference in practicing law in Rawhide and New York City," Isabella pointed out.

"Nick practiced corporate law with one of the most important law firms in Denver. So he's not entirely inexperienced."

"Okay."

But she didn't seem completely reassured.

After lunch they returned to the office where the marriage licenses were acquired. Isabella was a little embarrassed, but Russ wasn't. After they got the marriage license, he asked about the form to fill out to apply for adoption. The woman handed it over with instructions.

Then they were on their way back to Rawhide.

"I hope Sarah didn't have any difficulties with Angel," Isabella said, worrying her bottom lip.

"Angel? I'm sure she was perfect."

Isabella laughed. "I think I took advantage of your innocence."

He smiled at her, showing no worry. "No, I know babies can be a problem. I've even heard Rich and I were a handful. Once, when we were about four years old, all our folks went to Hawaii, leaving us in the care of Red and his wife Mildred and Uncle Griffin and Aunt Camille before they got married. There were five of us little ones, and Toby was in elementary school. One of us came down with chicken pox and quickly spread it around. In the meantime, Red and Mildred had an emergency and left before they knew about the pox. That left Camille to cope, with Griffin's help. Until he got chicken pox, too."

"Oh, my, that's dangerous. That poor woman. How did she manage?"

"Doc helped, and she hired some ladies to come clean up after us. Once the parents got wind of it, they all came home. So, see, my family knows about hard times."

"I guess they do."

When they stopped at Nick and Sarah's, Angel was sleeping soundly.

"Oh, she was wonderful, Isabella. If you need me to keep her while you're on your honeymoon, I can," Sarah offered.

Isabella looked as if Sarah had slapped her. ''Honeymoon?''

''We'll postpone that for a while, Sarah,'' Russ said quickly. ''With her great-aunt having just died and the move from New York to here, Isabella's got enough adjusting to do.''

''That's true. I only had to move across the street and it wasn't easy.''

''But...but the general store is across the street,'' Isabella said. ''You lived there?''

''Yes. That's my family's store. I ran it when my father died, and my sister and I lived on the second floor. Now my manager lives there.''

''Oh. That worked out well.''

Sarah looked at her husband, laughing. ''Yes, it did.''

''Don't let her fool you,'' Nick said. ''She had her doubts.''

Isabella nodded, an understanding look in her eyes.

Russ grinned. ''The important thing is you gave it a try, Sarah. Now, we're on our way to the ranch. Isabella and Angel are going to stay there until the wedding.''

''We will be invited, won't we?'' Sarah asked. ''I guess it will be small, but we are family.''

''Oh, I doubt we'll have any guests, Sarah. We'll just find a justice of the peace to marry us.'' Isabella looked at Russ to agree with her description of their coming wedding.

Russ laughed, enjoying her confusion. ''She

hasn't encountered the Randall women as a whole. Nor does she know how much they can accomplish in three days. I'm sure you'll be invited."

Isabella waited until they were in the truck again, with Angel strapped in between them. "Russ, surely we won't have a guest list with three days' notice."

"Are you against guests? My family does things in a big way. They're not going to want it to look like they're not happy about our marriage."

"They probably *aren't* happy, truth be told. I'm sure they think I'm taking advantage of you."

Russ sobered. "No, they're going to be grateful to you. I've come back to life, and that's what they wanted."

"Was it that bad?" she asked.

"I haven't been to the ranch but once in the last eighteen months, Isabella. I hid from life. It was cowardly of me, but it was all I could manage. I hadn't laughed, either. But now I'm living again. You know I'm not marrying you because I've fallen in love with you. I wouldn't mislead you. But I'll take care of the two of you. I'll be a good husband."

"Yes. I'll try to be a good wife like…like that. A partnership. That's what we'll have."

"Exactly."

ISABELLA'S FIRST GLIMPSE of the Randall ranch was a surprise. There were a lot of buildings, as well as a large house.

"How many people live in the house?"

"Ten adults and two children most of the time."

"Who does that include besides your parents? Red and Mildred?" She'd been paying attention.

"Nope. Red and Mildred live in that house to the left of the third barn. That's where B.J., Toby and Mildred lived when they first moved to the ranch. After Jake and B.J. married, Red and Mildred married and they moved to the other house to have a little privacy. No, Toby and Elizabeth are the other couple, with their two babies."

"How old are the babies?"

"The oldest, a boy, is three. The baby is a year old, just about three months older than Rich and Samantha's little one."

"Oh."

"Don't worry. Angel is going to fit right in."

"I hope so."

He could hear the concern in her voice. "She already has more hair than all of them."

Isabella ran her hand protectively over her baby's curls and said nothing.

After Russ parked the car, he took Angel's carrier from Isabella and guided both females into the big kitchen.

All the introductions were made, with help from various family members. Toby was the only member of the household who hadn't quit work early to meet her. Elizabeth apologized, explaining he was on a deadline with the horse he was training, but Isabella told her she wasn't offended.

"I'm sorry the rest of you thought you should stop work just to meet us."

Janie, unable to hold back, hugged her. "We're so pleased to meet you. I told them all how beautiful you were. But Angel is even prettier than I described. Those curls are spectacular."

"Janie's excited because she's never had a baby girl to buy for. She's got a daughter-in-law, of course, but all her babies have been boys," B.J. said.

"May I hold her?" Janie asked, hovering over the sleeping baby.

"Mom!" Russ protested. "Let her sleep. She'll be up in about fifteen minutes if she's on schedule."

"I have a bottle ready," Isabella said hurriedly. "She's very noisy when she's hungry."

That statement brought a lot of smiles.

"Come sit down. We have so much to ask you." Janie guided Isabella over to the big table.

Isabella shot a worried look at Russ. He knew she thought his mom's questions would be about her family and her past life, but Russ didn't think so. They had already made plans for the wedding.

The men excused themselves to go back to work.

"They stopped work just to say hello?" Isabella asked, surprised.

"If you want them to stay, they will, but they're not interested in discussing wedding plans," Janie said, watching her.

''No! I mean, I wasn't complaining. I was feeling bad that I caused them such a disruption.''

At that, everyone laughed and the men left, except for Russ. He thought, from the look on Isabella's face, that she was glad he stayed.

''Let me take your coat,'' Janie said. Isabella had worn the mink, but she wasn't coat proud. She slipped out of it.

''I'll hang it in the hall closet. It's lovely.''

''Just put it anywhere. It doesn't matter.''

Again, tension relaxed. Russ realized that his mom thought he might be marrying a woman unwilling to get off her high horse.

''Mom, Izzy is not like the woman Uncle Brett got engaged to. Just relax,'' he said.

''I wasn't...'' Janie began. Then she looked sheepishly at her son. ''I'll admit, we were worried.''

''Do people call you Izzy?'' Anna asked.

''Yes. Isabella is too formal, I think. I'd be happy for you to call me Izzy.''

The women all smiled.

''But...was Russ talking about you, Anna?''

Everyone laughed then.

''No, not me. When I met Brett, he was already engaged to a senator's daughter.''

Megan added, ''She thought she was the most important person in the world.''

''And she hated living on the ranch,'' Janie said. ''We wanted to make sure Brett caught on to that fact, so we invited her for a visit before the wedding.''

Red brought a plate of cookies to the table, along with mugs of coffee. ''She was awful. Didn't want me to eat with the family.'' He plopped down beside Mildred.

''You don't mind, do you?'' Red asked Isabella.

She smiled at Red. ''Of course not.''

Red sighed. ''Yep. This is gonna work out fine.''

''Now, our first question is changing the date of the wedding,'' Janie said. She suddenly had a piece of paper in front of her with writing all over it.

Before Isabella could say anything, Russ spoke. ''We have a difficulty that makes it necessary—''

''I'm only talking about postponing it until Saturday. That would be much better for our guests.''

''Isabella didn't think we'd have any guests,'' Russ couldn't resist saying with a grin.

His mother stared at him, tears suddenly in her eyes.

Isabella rushed in to say, ''I'm sorry. I didn't think—''

Janie wiped her eyes. ''It's not that, dear. I...I haven't seen Russ smile in so long.''

''Mom!'' Russ protested, embarrassed by his mother's behavior.

Isabella remembered his words in the truck. ''Maybe you'd better go away, so I can hear all the women's ideas. I think I'm going to like them.''

''The women or the ideas?'' Russ asked.

"Both!" she replied, a big smile on her lips. A beautiful smile.

Russ hadn't seen her smile like that until now. A good thing. He would've agreed to anything if she'd looked like that. And she even had her hair pinned down in that French knot again.

"Okay, I'll go. But whatever else you decide, I want your hair down on your shoulders when we get married." Then he got up, accompanied by Red, and headed for one of the barns.

ISABELLA WAS AFRAID she'd done something wrong. Everyone was silent. "I'm sorry. Did you want him to stay?"

Janie squeezed her hand. "Oh, no, honey, nothing's wrong. Everything's right. I haven't seen Russ act like he was alive in so long."

"Mrs. Randall—"

Everyone protested. B.J. spoke for all of them. "We banned formality a long time ago, Izzy. We all answer to that title. Stick to first names and there's no confusion."

"I see. Janie, our marriage is not…not like his marriage with Abby. You may feel I'm taking advantage of him when you understand why we're getting married."

Everyone leaned in closer. "We're all ears," Elizabeth, Toby's wife, said, "but I doubt you'll convince us. It's such a joy to have Russ back. I've got to call Samantha. She and Rich will be so pleased!"

Isabella wanted to make them all happy, but she had to tell the truth. "I need a family for Angel. And Russ fell for Angel. He wants to be her daddy."

"Are you going somewhere?" Janie asked, confusion on her face.

"My father is going to be very angry with me."

The implications were obvious to everyone.

Mildred stared at her. "You mean you think he would hurt you?"

Isabella licked her lips. "Hopefully not if Nick does his job well. I'm making sure the inheritance I received from Aunt Maria can never be taken by my father."

There were several questions and Isabella answered them as honestly as she could, until Janie asked a more difficult question.

"But how do you feel about Russ?"

Isabella had been open, and now they all watched as that openness disappeared. Cautiously, she said, "I think Russ and I will be good friends. He's a…a good person, and he'll be a great father for Angel."

"Nicely said," B.J. replied. "Are you still mourning Angel's father?"

"No! Not at all. I'm ashamed to say it, but I married him to spite my father. I thought he would stand up to my father. Instead, after about six months, he sold out for a sports car that killed him. I was four months pregnant at the time."

The women all looked at each other and nodded. Then Janie said, "Welcome to the family."

"You don't mind? I mean, I promise to try to make Russ happy."

"Good. Wear your hair loose at the wedding. He's right. It's gorgeous. It's like the baby's except much longer," Janie said to the others. "It will be spectacular."

"But I don't have anything to wear. There's a yellow dress, but it's for summer."

"How about my wedding gown?" Elizabeth asked. "We're about the same height. Mildred does wonderful tailoring."

Before Isabella knew what was happening, she found herself up the stairs, trying on a beautiful white gown. Janie got on the phone and ordered a tux for both her sons, since she figured Rich would be Russ's best man.

B.J., Megan and Anna began planning the meal they would serve to the neighborhood. Suggestions flew fast and furious.

"But…I mean, there's snow everywhere. Where can we have that many people for dinner?" Isabella asked.

"In the arena. You'll see. It's where Toby and Elizabeth got married," B.J. explained.

Isabella nodded, but she had no idea where or, just what the "arena" was. Yet she was glad she'd turned her life over to these women. They were wonderful.

Then Angel, in the carrier on the bed in the room Isabella had been given, announced her feeding time. Everyone flew to the carrier, and Isabella got to show off her pride and joy. They all thought Angel was beautiful. Just another reason to realize how fortunate she was.

Chapter Eight

Russ flipped on the kitchen light as he entered his apartment. Tonight was different.

Angel and Isabella weren't here.

It was really Angel he missed, of course, but he couldn't have Angel without Isabella. That was why he'd included Isabella in that thought. He should be glad she wasn't here. He'd get to sleep in his own bed tonight.

He should change the sheets, but he was tired. He'd had a long day. Somehow, jumping back into the family activities had taken a lot out of him. But he couldn't leave Isabella on her own. So he'd stayed all afternoon, visiting with Red. Then he'd stayed for dinner, sitting beside Isabella at the family table, interacting with everyone.

He even stayed for Angel's ten-o'clock feeding. Isabella had let him feed her, but she'd sat beside him, her scent encircling him and the baby.

Angel had been particularly sweet. After she'd finished her bottle, Isabella and he had talked to her.

The baby had listened intently, her gaze moving from one to the other. Izzy had burped her. Then she'd placed Angel in a baby bed and Russ had spread a blanket over her.

He'd bent over and kissed the baby good-night. Then he'd turned to Isabella. It had seemed natural to place a kiss on her cheek, too. Her skin was almost as soft as the baby's, but the temptation to kiss Isabella's lips had surprised him. He'd beat a fast retreat.

Russ checked the thermometer. The place seemed cold. No wonder. It was close to zero outside. He stepped into the kitchen and put on some water to boil. A cup of instant decaf would help settle him down.

He couldn't have gotten so used to Isabella and her baby in the few days they'd stayed with him. And Saturday night, they'd be back together again. Forever.

He made his cup of coffee and headed for his bedroom. Isabella had been very neat. There was almost no trace of her. He sat on the edge of his bed and took a sip of coffee. Then he realized what he was smelling. Isabella had left her scent in his room. It made it impossible to forget her warmth, to forget her. If he stayed in there he feared she'd invade his dreams and he'd lose all control of his feelings.

Suddenly he stood and returned to the living room. Turning on the television, he settled on the couch. He was more comfortable there than in his bedroom.

When he awoke the next morning, he was still on the sofa with the television playing.

He went down to the office after he'd showered, shaved and changed. He found Bill Wilson already there. "Bill! I didn't expect you this early."

"It's not like I had to crawl through the snow, Russ."

Russ laughed. Bill, Jon's father, rented the apartment next to his and worked at the accounting firm with Tori and Russ. "I guess I don't have that excuse, either. Did your wife try to make it out to Gabe's ranch?" Bill's wife worked during the day as Gabe and his wife Jennifer's housekeeper.

"She talked about it, but Gabe told her not to try. He was staying in with his wife and babies today. So I told her to make us a good lunch."

"Does that 'us' include me?"

"It does."

"Good. Uh, by the way, Bill, I should tell you I'm getting married this Saturday." He watched as Bill stared at him in surprise.

"Who are you marrying?"

"You don't know her. I found her and her baby in the blizzard and rescued them. Her baby is six weeks old and called Angel. Isabella was sick and I took care of Angel and fell in love with her."

"Good for you, Russ." Bill shook his head. "We've all been worried about you, but we couldn't figure out what to do. God worked it out by Himself."

"Yeah, I guess He did."

The front door opened and Tori hurried in. "Hi. Brisk this morning, isn't it?"

Both men greeted her. But her return greeting was a surprise. She put her arms around Russ's neck and hugged him. "I'm so happy for you."

"Ah. The family gossips have been busy," Russ said with a wry grin.

"Your mother is up on the roof shouting hooray." Tori proceeded past him to her office. "I've got a lot to get done today."

"Uh, I have to talk to you about something." Russ moved to the door of her office. "Mind if I come in?"

She waved him in. He spoke to Bill, then entered Tori's office and closed the door. "It turns out that Isabella inherited majority stock holdings in the family company. She wants to leave it all to Angel, of course, with me as guardian. She was going to leave money to pay me for my work, and I protested. Nick suggested she put you in charge of the trust fund and you would be paid for your efforts. That okay with you?"

Tori blinked several times. "Well, I guess so. What's the name of the company?"

"Paloni Industries. I don't know anything about it."

"I've seen the name, but I never connected it to Maria Paloni. She had me make some investments for her, so I knew she wasn't hurting, but..." While she talked, she was punching buttons on her computer. Then she whistled under her breath. "How much did she own?"

"I don't know exactly. More than fifty percent."

"That's a big conglomerate. It's publicly held, but most of the stock is held by the founding family. We're talking millions of dollars."

"I gathered."

"Well, you're going to be the richest man in Rawhide."

"Not me. My wife."

"Same thing. Is she going to sell?"

"I don't think so. She thinks her father will do anything to gain control. And it seems she doesn't want to do him any favors."

"This sounds serious. Does she think he'll threaten her?"

"She thinks he'll kill her."

Tori gasped. Then she firmed her lips. "She needs to sell the stock. The sooner the better."

"I don't think she will. It's a family company."

"Suddenly I'm not so thrilled about your marriage."

"It won't affect me." Russ smiled. "I'm involved to keep Angel safe."

"Yeah, right! You're telling me if a man comes after Isabella, you're not going to protect her?"

Russ paced the short distance across the office. Then he shrugged. "I probably will. But Angel's going to stay in the family. She won't be going back to her grandfather. So it won't matter in the long run.''

''It matters to us if something happens to you!'' Tori snapped.

''I don't think it will come to that. I think Isabella's father threatens a lot and has never had to prove he means it.''

''I'll take care of the trust, but watch your back.''

This time Russ hugged Tori. ''Don't worry. If I get lost I can count on you and Jon coming to find me, can't I?''

''Probably, unless I'm pregnant again.''

''Pregnant? Do you think you are?''

''Not yet, but Jonny is eight months old. Within the next year we'll probably have another baby.''

''Then I'll have to take care of myself. I'm not risking a niece or nephew's life,'' he assured her with a grin.

''Don't take this too lightly, Russ,'' Tori warned.

''No, I won't. I'm going to get to work. Nick will contact you about the trust.''

He slipped out of his cousin's office and into his. Bill was working at his desk and didn't even look up. Once he was behind his desk, Russ called Nick.

''Tori okayed the trust idea,'' he said at once.

''Good. I had a call from Mr. Paloni this morning.''

''What did he say?''

''I had my secretary give him a message that I would be out of the office until Monday due to a family wedding.''

"Clever. You think that will hold him?"

"Yeah. I'm pretty sure he thinks I don't have any idea what he's up to. Once he discovers I've taken precautions against him accomplishing his goal, all bets are off."

"Nick, do you really believe he'll harm Isabella?"

"I hope not, but you never can tell. By the way, we got a call this morning inviting us to the wedding. Sarah was pleased."

"I'm glad." Russ grimaced. "I've got to call Isabella and see if they've driven her crazy yet, taking over her life."

"Okay, I'll get with Tori, and we'll see you Saturday."

Russ hung up. He didn't dial the ranch right away. He was thinking about what Tori had said. He didn't believe money was worth anyone's death. Especially not Isabella's.

He drew a deep breath. Then he reached for the phone again.

Red answered and assured him Isabella was there at the breakfast table. When he heard her soft voice, he relaxed. "How's it going, Izzy?"

"Fine. Your family is wonderful."

"Told you you were getting a good bargain."

"Yes. Are you okay? Did you enjoy getting back in your bed last night?"

"Sure," he lied. "How's Angel? On schedule?"

"Actually the mothers thought I should increase her milk another two ounces. Janie called Jon at home and he agreed it wouldn't hurt. I did and she's sleeping six hours now. That means I'll only have to get up once a night.''

''Okay. And you don't resent my mother taking over your life?''

Isabella laughed, a sound Russ enjoyed. ''Your mother, and all the mothers, are so kind. They try very hard not to interfere, but then they can't help themselves. I love it. My mother died when I was very young. I missed so much. I'm so grateful to you, Russ. Please don't tell me you've changed your mind.''

''No! Of course not. I was afraid you might've changed yours.''

''No, never.''

''Listen, Isabella, I'm worried about your father. I think you should just give the stock to him and put him out of your life. Money isn't worth your life.''

''I probably exaggerated the danger, Russ. My father and I don't have a good relationship.''

''I figured that out.''

She gave an edgy laugh. ''I need some time to think things through, Russ. We'll work it out.''

''Okay. Say, do you know how to ride?''

''That was a quick change of subject. No, I can't ride.''

''I want to teach you. What size jeans do you wear?''

''That's a very personal question,'' she said.

''Honey, marriage is even more personal.''

There was a long silence and Russ remembered that their marriage was going to be different. He was about ready to tell her to forget it when she said abruptly, ''I wear a size ten.''

''Boot size?''

''I guess a size seven. That's my shoe size.''

''Okay. Tell Red I'll be eating with everyone tonight. And I'll be out there around four. Okay?''

''I don't think we eat that early.''

''I'm coming early to spent time with my new family.''

''Oh.''

TORI WENT HOME at two, something she'd begun when she returned to work after Jonny's birth. If she had to stay longer, she'd brought her baby in after lunch and put him to bed in her office.

When she'd gone, Russ told Bill he was going to the general store across the street. ''When I get back, I'll probably go out to the ranch. If you want to quit early, feel free. You shouldn't have to be the only one working.''

Bill shook his head. ''I want to get finished with this part of the books on the café. Then I'll call it quits.''

When Russ entered the store, he asked the female clerk to help him find jeans and boots for Isabella. First they looked at boots. Russ chose some black leather boots with a simple design on the upper part of them. She recommended he buy a half-size larger because of the instep. Then they added out some jeans.

"Does she need anything else? Gloves, a jacket?"

"Damn, I almost forgot. Yeah, she'll need a ski jacket. Something in blue." He wanted it to match her eyes. "And maybe a hat, too, and gloves."

A half hour later, his arms full of packages, he walked to his truck. He put all the packages on the passenger side. Then he circled the truck and slid behind the wheel.

He hoped the jeans fit. He'd pictured Isabella in the new additions to her wardrobe. He couldn't wait to see her wearing her cowboy hat. Of course, he'd bought all that so Izzy would get acclimated to horseback riding. Then, when Angel got a little older and he wanted to teach her how to ride, Izzy wouldn't protest.

When he reached the house, he found everyone working on some project for the wedding. "I thought you would keep it simple since there's not much time," he protested.

"Nonsense. We want your wedding to be as nice as…" Janie stopped and started again. "We want it as nice as any of the Randall weddings. Besides, most of the weddings have happened in a hurry."

Russ and Abby had planned their wedding for almost a year. Then Rich and Samantha had joined them at the last minute. He just shook his head. "Where is Isabella? With Angel?"

"No, but before you find her, I want to talk to you."

"What about?"

"Inviting her family to the wedding."

"Absolutely not!" Russ said adamantly.

"But, son, isn't there anyone in her family that's nice?"

"I think Angel's pretty agreeable. We could invite her."

"Well, of course, she'll be there," Janie exclaimed. "But I feel badly Isabella has no one else."

"She's got us, Mom, and we're more than enough for anyone." He changed the subject. "Now, where's Isabella?"

"Isabella went to her great-aunt Maria's house with Megan and Mildred and Angel is asleep in Isabella's room."

"What? But I told her I'd be here at four."

Janie raised an eyebrow. "Does that mean she's supposed to be here waiting for you?"

"Well, yes."

"It's not four yet. She still has twenty minutes before she's late. And sometimes things happen."

Russ felt betrayed by his future wife. She should've been there. He was anxious to see her—to assure himself everything was okay. Of course it wasn't that he missed her. Or longed to see her for herself. He just wanted everything to flow smoothly. He knew he was lying to himself, but he didn't want to admit his weakness for Isabella. That would make him too vulnerable.

Red, who'd been working at the sink on something, poured a couple of cups of coffee and brought one to Russ. "Here, boy. Sit down and talk to me. I need a little masculine companionship. These women are running around like chickens with their heads cut off."

"Thanks, Red." Russ took the coffee and sat. Then he said, "I could run over to her aunt's house and see what's holding them up."

"You'd probably pass them on the way. Is the snow melting any? It'd be nice if it went away before Saturday. In fact, we should walk down to the arena to see if you approve of what they've done down there," Red suggested.

"Okay, sure." He figured he could hear the car returning more easily down there than he could shut up in the house.

"Remember, Mom, no talking to Isabella's family. It will just be Randalls on Saturday. You promise?"

"I promise." But he could see she still wasn't happy about it.

"I'll leave these packages here, okay?"

"Okay. What are they?"

"Cowboy gear for Isabella."

"I'll keep an eye on them." Janie watched as her son and Red left the house. So he was only marrying Isabella because of the baby? But it was Isabella he was impatient to see, not the baby. And it was Isabella for whom he'd bought cowboy gear. Janie was feeling better about this marriage with every passing minute. But she wished they'd agree to invite Izzy's family.

"OH, MY, I HAD NO IDEA there would be so much work involved," Isabella protested as she collapsed in a stuffed chair.

"I know," Megan agreed. "We've finally finished the living room, but we have a lot more rooms to work on. And there's so much stuff. I don't know where we'll store it."

Mildred nodded. "Though I sure wouldn't mind buying that painting of the mountains."

"Oh, Mildred, please take it. You've all been so good to me. I was afraid...I mean, I didn't think you would welcome me like you have."

"And why wouldn't we?" Mildred challenged. "Not only are you sweet and beautiful, but you make Russ want to live again."

"It's not me. It's Angel. While I was sick, he took complete care of her. Then, as I got better, I had to fight just to get to feed her," she told them with a smile on her lips. "He's promised to keep my baby safe."

"You, too, I hope," Megan said.

"I don't want him to get hurt," Isabella said.

"What is it your father wants so badly?" Megan asked.

"My aunt owned the majority of shares in the family company. She gave him the power of attorney, so he controlled her vote. Now that I've inherited the shares, he'll want my power of attorney. I don't trust him.''

''Ah. A power struggle. Sounds dangerous to me.''

''I know. And Russ said I should just give the shares to him. But that would be giving away Angel's birthright.''

''And letting him win,'' Mildred added.

''Yes,'' Isabella agreed, nodding firmly. ''That's not right.''

''No, but it might be smarter. We want you and Angel to be safe. And Russ, too.''

''I know,'' Isabella said. ''That's my dilemma.''

''Well, if you're going to be there when Russ arrives, we'd better hurry back to the ranch,'' Mildred said. ''It's ten till four already.''

Mildred couldn't have said anything that got Isabella moving faster than that. Both women noticed her eagerness to see Russ again. They figured it was a good sign.

Chapter Nine

Red watched as Russ ran out of the barn at the sound of a car, their conversation completely forgotten.

He followed Russ and stood with Megan and Mildred as Russ grabbed Isabella's hand and tugged her toward the house. "Wait until you see what I bought you."

"But you shouldn't have bought me anything, Russ."

"Yes, I should've. You'll need them."

The pair disappeared into the house.

"Well, well, well, so he's marrying for the baby's sake, is he?" Red said.

"That's what he says," Mildred said. "That's what she says, too. But when I told her she'd be late, she rushed around like the house was on fire."

"I think Janie's right. I think Russ cares about Isabella, but he's afraid to admit it," Megan said.

"Yep," Red agreed. "Let's follow them. We've got to start dinner."

Once inside the house, they found Janie at the table, but no sign of Russ and Isabella. ''Where did the kids go?'' Red asked.

''Upstairs to try on her new things,'' Janie said, seemingly satisfied with their action.

''We all agree with you about what's going on,'' Mildred said.

''Good. Oh, Red, I invited Rich, Samantha and Mom over for dinner.'' Janie smiled. ''I gave them my opinion about what's going on.''

''I hope you told them not to say anything,'' Red said.

''Of course.''

''RUSS, I CAN'T come out,'' Isabella called through the door.

''Why not? I want to see you in the jeans.''

''They're too tight, Russ. I guess I've gained weight since I got to Rawhide.''

He knew better than that. She'd only eaten for the past couple of days. And then not much. ''Open the door and let me see,'' he ordered.

She finally opened the door a couple of inches. From the way she'd talked, he'd expected to find the jeans unsnapped. But they fit her perfectly. He pushed the door all the way open. ''You look great!''

''Russ! I'm afraid to bend over. They'll split if I do.''

''No. That's the way they're supposed to fit. Now let's try on the boots.''

"But I don't have any socks. I'll have to—"

"Mom!" Russ called down the stairs. "We need a pair of socks for Izzy."

"Russ! I have socks, but—"

"You need thick ones for the boots. Here comes Mom. She'll get you some."

Isabella tried to close the door. "I don't want her to see me! These jeans are too tight."

"Mom, tell Isabella her jeans aren't too tight. They look great." Russ motioned his mother over.

"They do look good, Isabella," Janie said. "We all wear our jeans a little tighter than your tailored pants." She went into her room and came out with a pair of thick socks. "These should work with the boots. Oh, I invited Rich and Samantha and your grandmother for dinner tonight, Russ." Then she disappeared back down the stairs.

"I thought your grandmother was dead," Isabella said, distracted from her difficulties.

"This is my mother's mother. You'll like her. She lives with Rich and Samantha on her ranch, the one Rich and I and Casey will inherit. Rich runs it."

"Oh. Is it big?"

"Fair size."

"Does that mean you'll quit your job?"

"Gosh, no! Rich does a good job of running it. I might go help during roundup each year, but he managed this year without me." He guided her to the bed. "Sit down and I'll put your socks on you."

"I can do that."

"Yeah, but I'm going to do it. Cute toes," he said as his warm hand cupped one foot. Her toenails were painted pink, like her fingernails.

"Th-thank you."

After he had that sock on, he took the boot for that foot and pulled out the packing material. He flexed the boot to loosen it up a little. Then he ordered, "Slide your foot inside."

She had to stand up to do as he asked. After a struggle, she got her foot completely inside the boot. "I suppose you wear these tighter than normal shoes, too."

"It just feels like it because they're closed in. Sit back down and we'll get the other one on." He slid the sock on and then presented the boot. She put one hand on his shoulder as she stood and slid her foot in. "Okay," she said, a little breathless, "I've got them on. What are the other packages?"

"Well, you can't wear your mink coat on a horse, so I bought you a ski jacket. It's blue to match your eyes." He held it out for her. Then he opened the last package and plopped a black Stetson hat on her head.

"I need a cowboy hat? Why?"

"I started to get you a knit cap, but when the sun's shining down on you, you need the shade. Or if it's raining or snowing, you need it, too."

"Why would you ride if it's raining or snowing?"

"You might not have a choice. Weather can change quickly. You have to be prepared." He stepped back and studied her critically. Then he smiled. ''Perfect.''

''What?'' she asked him, a little confused.

''You,'' he said succinctly. Then he stepped forward and dropped a kiss on her lips.

''Russ!'' she protested.

''We'll have to do that at the wedding. I thought we should practice beforehand, that's all. Besides, you look real cute as a cowgirl.'' He took her hand. ''Let's go show everyone.''

Reluctantly, she followed him.

All the mothers and Mildred and Red were in the kitchen. B.J. had just come back from doing vet work and was dressed quite similarly to Isabella, which relieved Isabella's mind about how appropriately she was dressed.

''You look wonderful, Izzy,'' Janie said.

''I feel rather bizarre,'' she said, slanting a look at Russ.

He simply grinned. Then he said to the others, ''We're going to the arena to give Izzy her first riding lesson.''

''Dinner is at six, boy, so don't be late,'' Red warned.

''I figure she'll only manage an hour today, Red. I don't want her to get too sore.'' Russ took Isabella's hand as he spoke and started pulling her toward the door. She almost tripped on the boots, since she wasn't used to walking in them.

''Son, take things slowly, okay?''

''Sure, Mom.'' He agreed cheerfully, not slowing down at all.

Isabella gave them all a fleeting wave, apprehension on her face.

''YOU'VE NEVER BEEN on a horse?'' Russ asked again as they strode down a path to one of the larger buildings.

''No. I've seen the police riding them, that's all.''

''Okay, we'll start by introducing you to some horses. You want to see the babies first?''

''You have babies? Yes, I want to see the babies.''

They entered the second barn. ''This is where we put the mamas when it's time. I think Red said this one was born yesterday.''

Isabella looked over the half door and saw a mare with a tiny, fragile-looking horse only a couple of feet tall standing next to her.

''Oh,'' she said, letting go of some of her fears, ''he's beautiful.''

''She. This is a filly.''

''Can I pet her?''

''Probably not. She's her mama's first baby. They're both a little nervous.''

Russ tugged Isabella along to the next stall. ''This lady is an old hand at having babies. Besides, the baby is almost a week old. We wouldn't have him in here except for the early snowstorm. You can pet him.''

This foal was a little bigger and seemed much more comfortable on his wobbly legs. Isabella reached over the door to pet him, but he was too far away.

Russ undid the gate, startling her. "Don't let them out!" she protested.

"I'm not, honey. I'm letting you in."

She took a step back. "You want me to go in there? The mother is so big. What if she gets angry?"

"I'm going with you. I'll protect you." He led the way into the stall. "Hello, Marmie," he said softly, rubbing the mare's nose.

"Her name is Marmie?"

"No. Her name is Marmalade. Come rub her nose. It's very soft."

"But I wanted to pet her baby."

"You have to make friends with her mother first. Take off your gloves." He took them from her and stuck them in her coat pocket. "Now, reach out and rub her nose."

She hesitantly did so. "She won't bite me?"

"Nope, not Marmie. We have a few horses that might do that, but not her."

Isabella rubbed her hand back and forth. "You're right. Her nose is very soft."

"Yeah. Now that you've got his mama's scent on you, the colt might let you pet him." He reached out slowly to the colt and put a firm hand on his back. "Try him."

She stretched her hand out and gently rubbed the

colt's nose even as he stepped back toward his mother. The mare moved several steps, too, which scared Isabella and she jumped back, landing against Russ's solid body.

"Easy there. You're okay."

"I th-think I've petted him enough." She pressed even closer to Russ.

He put his arm around her and moved them both out of the stall. "You did fine for the first time. Did you like it?"

"Yes, but the mother is so big! What if she steps on me?"

Russ grinned at her. "You'll walk with a limp for a few days."

"Oh."

She looked so worried, even though they'd left the stall, he couldn't resist kissing her. His lips touched hers, and this kiss was a little longer, a little more intimate and definitely hotter than the last kiss.

He turned her around and pulled her against him, and he kissed her again. When he raised his head, he said, "What's wrong? Don't you like it?"

"It's very nice, but…but it worries me."

"Why does it worry you?"

"We're not supposed to…to…you know."

"We didn't say we couldn't. Just that we weren't planning on it. But we're going to be married a long time. Are we going to do without for the rest of our lives?"

"I hadn't thought about it."

''Well, I think you'd better think about it. Because if you don't like me kissing you, you probably won't like anything else.''

Isabella gave him a quick look. Then she stepped away. ''I didn't say I didn't like it. But I've had a lot of changes. I just hadn't thought... Do we have to right away?''

''No, I guess not. Come on, let's go put you on a horse.''

''Why?''

''How else will you learn to ride?''

''Why do I have to learn to ride?''

''Well, when Angel grows some and we're going on a camping trip, are you going to want to stay at home every time?''

''Can't we go camping in a truck?''

He took her hand and pulled her to the door of the barn. Then he put his hands on her shoulders and turned her toward the ridge of mountains that ran along the western horizon. ''See those mountains? That's where we like to go camping. A truck can't get up them. There are no roads.''

''Oh. But can't we take things more slowly? I have so much to worry about that I can't think about horses now.''

He ran his hands through his hair. ''I didn't realize it required so much thought.''

''It's hard to learn new things when you're an adult.'' She shivered in the cold air.

''Okay, I guess we can wait until after we're

married. After all, Angel isn't likely to ask to go camping in the next two years."

"But when she's three, she will? I don't think that will happen. And even if it does, I won't let her go when she's that young."

"You're not going to mollycoddle her, are you?"

"What does that mean, mollycoddle?"

"It means treat her like a baby."

Isabella frowned at him, her hands on her hips. "She *is* a baby. Of course I'm going to treat her like one!"

"I don't want her to be afraid of her own shadow."

"And I don't want her to get hurt!"

"I'm not going to hurt her. What's the matter with you?"

"Nothing's wrong with me! You're the crazy one, the one not keeping his promises! I'm beginning to think I've made a huge mistake!"

By now they were both shouting.

"If you think you've made a mistake, just take your baby and go. I'm certainly not going to hold you to anything!"

"Fine! I will!" She pushed her way out of the barn and stomped down the path in her new boots.

"Fine!" Russ hollered after her. "See if I care!" He was determined this woman was not going to hurt him.

Halfway to the house, he was joined by his twin

brother and his wife, Samantha. "Hey, Russ. Congratulations. Mom told us the good news."

"Don't congratulate me! The wedding is off!"

Rich and Samantha came to a halt, staring at Russ, who continued to the house.

ISABELLA WAS DEVASTATED. She dashed into the kitchen, tears running down her cheeks, forgetting about all the people in the house.

She was halfway through the kitchen when reality hit her. "Oh!" That made the tears fall harder and she ran for the bedroom she'd used the night before. Though, if she was breaking off the marriage with Russ, they probably wouldn't want her there any longer.

She had no place to go. No one to help her. It would just be her and Angel against the world. She cried even more.

She fell across the bed, trying to keep her sobs quiet so she wouldn't wake the baby.

"Izzy? Come in to our room so you won't wake the baby," Janie said softly, taking her arm to guide her.

She'd obviously followed Isabella up the stairs.

Isabella was scarcely conscious of movement. She didn't know what to do or where to go, but someone did. That was a comforting thought.

"What's wrong?" Janie asked as she and Isabella entered her room. The other three Randall women were there, waiting for them.

‘‘Russ refuses to marry me because I can’t ride a horse.’’

Isabella fell into a chair, covering her face.

‘‘But I thought he was going to teach you,’’ Megan said.

‘‘I didn’t want to learn now. I’m...I’m scared of horses.’’

She sobbed several times. ‘‘He said he and Angel would go camping without me. I said I wouldn’t let Angel go and he yelled at me!’’

‘‘The beast!’’ Janie said, biting her bottom lip.

Surprised by Janie’s sympathy, Isabella looked up to see laughter in Janie’s gaze. ‘‘I guess it wasn’t a good idea. I don’t think I can...he changed his mind. And I said not now. And...and he...’’

More tears.

‘‘He changed his mind about marrying you?’’ B.J. asked in surprise.

‘‘No. He changed his mind about...kissing and s-stuff.’’

‘‘And you said you weren’t ready to change the rules, and he got upset,’’ Megan added. ‘‘That’s what happened, wasn’t it?’’

‘‘How d-did you know?’’ Isabella asked in surprise. ‘‘And I have to leave now. I can’t stay here if there’s not going to be a wedding. That wouldn’t be right. But I don’t know where to go or what to do.’’

‘‘Of course you don’t,’’ Janie said with a sigh, pulling Isabella into her arms. ‘‘But you’re wrong about leaving. You can stay here as a guest. As my friend.''

Isabella turned tragic eyes on Janie. ''No, I couldn't. That wouldn't be fair to Russ.''

Janie kissed her cheek. ''Yes, it would. Go back to your room and lie down. We'll go talk to Russ. You know, in spite of having been married, he doesn't understand women all that well. Abby just agreed with everything he said.''

''No wonder he doesn't like me,'' Isabella muttered under her breath as she headed back to her own room.

The women all looked at each other. ''The problem,'' Janie said, ''is that he likes her too much. He's thawing out fast and doesn't understand why she isn't.''

''The poor girl is under so much pressure. Can we explain it to him?'' Megan asked.

''Pete will.''

They headed downstairs for some masculine input.

DOWNSTAIRS, THINGS WERE just erupting. Russ said nothing about the argument when he came inside. His father headed across the room to ask him what he'd done to Isabella when Rich and Samantha entered the room and asked what had happened. That distracted Pete. By the time they had explained what they were asking, everyone turned to stare at Russ.

''What's wrong with you, boy?'' Red asked.

"That doesn't sound like you. And Isabella is so sweet."

"I don't want to discuss it," Russ said.

"But you're going to have to. Is the wedding off?" his father asked.

"Yes! She refuses to marry me. It's not my fault."

"Well, I think it is," Janie announced as she entered the room, followed by her sisters-in-law.

"Damn it! It's my life. Leave me alone!"

"We left you alone last time, and you lost eighteen months of living. Now, when you've finally come to your senses, you want us to give you up again?" Janie stared at her son. "Well, I won't do it. And I won't let you hurt Isabella."

"I'm not hurting her. She's hurting me!"

Pete stepped forward before his wife and son came to blows. "Russ, go to Jake's office. I'll be there in a minute to talk to you." When Pete used that tone of voice, his sons didn't argue with him.

Russ silently left the room.

Then Pete turned to his wife. "Come on, Janie. We need to have a little chat before I talk to Russ."

"Need any help?" Jake asked.

Pete smiled at his older brother. "I guess I'd better handle this one on my own."

"Russ might want me there," Rich said.

"You've been married almost two years. You think that makes you an expert?" Pete asked, grinning faintly.

''Nope. But Russ is my twin. If he's hurting, I want to help.''

''Okay, son. Go on into Jake's office and keep him company. I'll be there in a minute.''

Chapter Ten

When Pete walked into Jake's office, he found his twin sons chatting quietly.

"I'm glad you've calmed down, Russ. That was quite a scene you were creating out there."

"I'm sorry, Dad, but Isabella...she backed out of the marriage."

"Did she?"

"Yeah. She doesn't even like it when I kiss her!" His voice was rising again.

"Keep your voice down. I thought you promised that you would be friends, nothing else. Did you change your mind?"

"Hell, Dad, I promised to stay married to her forever, too. Was I supposed to do without any sex forever? That doesn't seem fair. Especially when she's so beautiful."

"I wondered about that."

"So what was I supposed to do?"

"He's got a point, Dad. His life would be miserable. He'd have to cheat on his marriage vows, or Isabella would have to—and she said she didn't want to,'' Rich protested, staunchly on his brother's side.

''Everyone draw a deep breath.'' Then Pete began his conversation where his wife said the difficulty had begun. ''Why did you decide to teach Isabella to ride today?''

''She doesn't know how.''

''She needs to know how to ride today?''

''Well, no, of course not, but eventually she will.''

''I agree, Dad,'' Rich added.

''Learning something new as an adult can be difficult. It requires a lot of energy and concentration,'' Pete pointed out. ''If a person, say, Isabella, had a lot of other problems to deal with, problems like her father trying to hurt her, taking care of a newborn baby, dealing with a husband who betrayed her and then died, moving away from home to a place where she didn't know anyone, mourning an aunt she'd never met who died before she could get here, being ill, you know, a few problems like that, do you think it would affect her willingness to take on something else? Other than marrying a stranger, I mean.''

''I forgot about all the problems she was facing.'' Russ ducked his head, embarrassed at his behavior.

''Not only that, son, but if she's not going to marry you, who's going to protect her from her father? Who will protect Angel? Do you think she'll let you? Do you think she'll stay here?''

Russ began to realize the enormity of what their argument had done. ''Damn! I didn't think. I just didn't think.''

''But, Dad,'' Rich said, ''he can't make that kind of promise! It just won't work.''

''I know that. But he could promise a year. He's gone eighteen months without any intimacy. I think he could wait a year, give Isabella a chance to settle in, resolve her issues with her father, let her feel at home here. She might look at everything differently then. Don't you agree, Russ?''

''Yeah. I... Things have been changing so quickly, I let myself get out of control. I'm sorry.''

''I don't think you need to apologize to me. But Isabella shed a few tears, you know.''

Taking a deep breath, Russ said, ''I'll go talk to her.''

''I knew you'd do the right thing, Russ. After you convince her, bring her down for dinner.''

''Yes, sir,'' Russ agreed before he left the room.

''Man, that was masterful,'' Rich muttered, thinking of his own role as father to his year-old son. ''I'm going to need to take lessons before Andy gets much older.''

''No hurry. Girls complicate life, yes, but Andy won't be interested in them for a while yet. You've got time. Let's go get us some dinner.''

ISABELLA HAD STOPPED crying. She lay on the bed, trying to make plans for the morning. She'd have to see if her car was ready. Russ had called someone after the blizzard stopped to have it towed and repaired. If it wasn't ready, she'd buy a new car.

She certainly couldn't hang around here. But she hated the thought of telling everyone goodbye.

A knock sounded on the door. She figured Janie was worried about her not eating. As if she could keep anything down. But she had to be polite. She slid off the bed and opened her door. Only to try to shut it again. She didn't want to talk to Russ.

"Sweetheart, I want to apologize," he pleaded.

"It's not necessary. Just go away."

"Not until I know you're okay...and you're still going to marry me."

"I can't."

"Why? Because you're afraid of horses? I shouldn't have pressed you on that. You have lots of time to learn how to ride. Or never to learn if you don't want to. And you have to marry me so I can take care of you and Angel. I promised."

"But I don't know if...I'm not ready to..."

"I know. We'll give it a year, after things have had plenty of time to settle. I won't pressure you in any way. We'll work something out. Okay?"

"And if we don't?"

"We will. Look, honey, I've been in the deep freeze for a long time. My life started changing so quickly I forgot things I'd learned. Like discipline, thinking about someone else's feelings, giving instead of taking. Things got out of hand today. But it won't happen again."

''I told you I was taking advantage of you. Now you know it's true.''

''No, it's not,'' he said. ''Today I was taking advantage of you. Forgive me?''

Tears filled her eyes. ''I'm sorry, too. I didn't mean to be difficult.''

''Lord have mercy. You're making me feel even worse.'' He put his arms around her and pulled her close.

She immediately stiffened.

''No, honey, I'm not trying to kiss you. I just want you to know I'm sorry.''

''It's okay.'' She eased out of his arms. ''Are you sure you want to go ahead with the wedding?''

''Yeah. It's going to be a big social event in Rawhide. We can't disappoint people,'' he added with a chuckle.

''That's not a good reason—''

''I was just trying to make it easier. We're going ahead for the best reason in the world. For Angel. We're going to take care of her, and we'll be happy, too. I'm sure of it. Now come downstairs and have some dinner.''

''Russ, I can't face all of them! What will they think?''

''They'll think I'm a monster. But if you want to eat up here, I'll go down and fix you a plate.''

''No. If you can face them, I can, too. I have to learn to be braver.''

''You set out on your own with a little baby, Isabella. I don't think your bravery is in question.

Come on.'' He took her hand and turned toward the door. Then he reached out a hand to smooth her hair and led her downstairs.

''Any food left?'' Russ asked as they entered the kitchen.

''Just a little,'' Red answered, grinning. ''Izzy, you make sure he serves you first. Otherwise, you won't get much.''

Her cheeks were red, but Isabella held her chin high. ''Russ will make sure I do. He's very thoughtful.''

He squeezed her hand. ''And she's very forgiving. The wedding's still on.''

Everyone cheered.

RUSS HELD HIMSELF together until he returned to his apartment. Then, alone, he had to face himself. He'd acted badly this evening. Because he wanted Isabella. He'd been lying to himself all along. Oh, he loved Angel and would enjoy being her daddy. But he'd felt an attraction to Isabella all along.

Once he'd kissed her, he'd felt an overpowering craving to touch her again. And the way he'd lived the past months had left him with no restraint. He was like a river breaking its banks and flowing wherever it wanted. He'd told himself he could never love again. But he was still alive. Very much so.

He'd thought Abby would never forgive him if he looked for happiness with another woman, but he'd been using her as an excuse because he was afraid of being hurt again.

Now it was too late. He wanted to be Isabella's husband in every sense of the word. But he'd promised.

So, as his father wisely said, he'd have to give Isabella time to adjust to Rawhide and their lifestyle. He'd have to wait until she dealt with her father. What if she decided to go back to New York? That thought bothered him. He'd suffer again. Could he convince her to stay here?

He didn't know. But he couldn't act as he had this afternoon. That much he knew. He'd been given a second chance, and he wasn't going to blow it.

THE NEXT FEW DAYS were busy. They moved a lot of the furniture out of the house Isabella had inherited from her great-aunt and hired some women to give it a thorough cleaning. Isabella discussed modernizing the kitchen with him. He voted for the same for the bathrooms.

It was a lovely old home, but it needed a lot of work. More insulation would be good, too. The furnace had a hard time keeping it warm. He packed some of his clothes the night before the wedding so he'd have changes of clothes there, but he left most of his things in the apartment.

Saturday morning Rich showed up on his doorstep.

"What are you doing here?" Russ asked.

"You haven't forgotten you're getting married today, have you?" Rich asked. "I'm your best man. I thought I should make sure you get to the ranch on time."

Russ grinned. "I'll be there. But since you're here, come on in. I've made a pot of coffee."

"Good. I picked up some cinnamon buns."

"Now I'm glad you came!" Russ teased as he stood back for his twin to enter. Soon they were seated at the table, enjoying their breakfast.

"Are you doing okay?" Rich asked. "I thought you might be having a hard time this morning."

"No, I'm okay." Russ chewed on the bun for several minutes. "I know Abby wouldn't have wanted me to live like I have. I certainly wouldn't want that for her. I think I was indulging in a long temper fit. But now I'm okay."

"Good. I wouldn't want to miss you again."

They shared a smile.

"I only have one other question," Rich continued.

"What's that?"

"You're not going to move to New York, are you?"

"No. And I'm going to try to convince Isabella not to do so, either. I don't think she and Angel would be safe there."

"You really think her father would harm either of them?"

"She's a stubborn woman. And their difficulty involves millions of dollars. Her father's ego is involved, too. She can take away his income and his job if she wants to.''

''When will he know she has that power?''

''Probably Monday.''

''Okay, we'll work out a schedule to stand guard.''

''I don't think he'll be vicious right away. He'll try to talk her into giving in to him. We can wait and see how he reacts.''

''You sure?''

''I think so.''

THE TWINS STOOD at the altar beside their pastor in the same church where the two of them were married in the same ceremony two and a half years ago. This time, only Russ would be getting married. But it felt eerily similar.

Elizabeth had volunteered to be matron of honor, wearing the bridesmaid dress she'd worn for a friend's wedding. The color was blue. It turned out to be Isabella's favorite color.

When the music began, Jake, who'd volunteered to escort the bride down the aisle, entered the church with Isabella on his arm. She'd followed Russ's wishes, wearing her hair down, the dark curls dancing on her shoulders under the veil.

She was beautiful.

Russ smiled at her, taking her hand as she and Jake reached him. Jake took his place on the second aisle across from Janie and Pete.

Isabella had a questioning look in her blue eyes,

and Russ squeezed her hand to reassure her. The minister led them through the ceremony. Russ was glad he'd cleared his mind about what he was doing. He could honestly repeat the vows now that he knew he wanted Isabella as his wife. Her fingers trembled in his as he slid the gold band he'd bought for her on her finger. But she managed to put his band on his finger. Her eyes had lit up when he'd shown her the matching bands.

Apparently she'd thought he wouldn't be willing to wear a ring. She looked up into his eyes as she said the last of the vows. He smiled reassuringly. Then they reached the best part.

"Russ, you may kiss your bride."

He slid his arms around her and his lips covered hers. The kiss was still as sweet as it had been the last time he kissed her, but he knew now it might be a while before he kissed her again, so he wasn't in any hurry.

Some applause broke out and he reluctantly released her. Her eyes were wide and she continued to stare at him until the minister turned them both toward the audience. "Ladies and gentlemen, I present to you Mr. and Mrs. Russell Randall. May God bless this union."

The wedding march began again and everyone stood and clapped. Russ led Isabella down the aisle and out the church to the limo his father had hired from Buffalo. Isabella's mink coat and his dress overcoat waited in the car for them. The driver closed the door, climbed into the front of the car and started the trip to the ranch.

"We did it," Isabella said in a disbelieving voice. "I didn't really think we would actually marry. Are you sure you aren't sorry?"

"No, sweetheart, I'm not sorry. We're going to do fine. And you don't have to whisper. He can't hear us unless I turn on the intercom."

"Should we have gotten Angel from your mom?"

"No, she'll bring her home to us."

"Did…did your mom tell you she asked me to call her Mom?"

"Izzy, you act like that will make me mad. That's wonderful."

"Yes. She…she's so sweet to me."

"She always wanted daughters." He wanted badly to kiss Isabella again, but he didn't dare. He might lose control. "Did you know Samantha is an orphan, too?" He laughed and added, "I guess technically you can't be called an orphan since your father is alive, but it's sort of the same."

"Yes, it is. I like Samantha. She told me all about her life until she met Rich. I wouldn't be nearly as brave as her being out on her own since she was sixteen. That was so young. And I imagine a rodeo life can be hard."

"Yes, it is, but you'd do what you have to do, like Samantha."

She was contemplating his response when her

stomach growled. "Oh, I'm sorry. I couldn't eat before the wedding and suddenly I'm hungry."

"There will be plenty of food at the ranch."

"I know. Red and Mildred have cooked nonstop for three days, and the others have pitched in part of the time. I'm amazed at how well they work together. It's so nice to see relatives living together and enjoying it."

"I told you you were getting a good family for Angel—and you."

"Yes, and you were right. You're very lucky."

He stared at her lips again. "I'm beginning to think so."

When they reached the ranch, moving at a purposely slow speed so the family and guests could arrive ahead of them, everything was ready. The limo pulled up beside the arena, and Russ escorted his beautiful bride into it. They'd built a temporary stage in the corral and they had tables lined up along the wall behind the stadiumlike seats.

The wonderful food aromas had Isabella staring at the tables with longing as they walked past.

"Not yet," Russ told her with a laugh. "First we have to greet our guests. Then we'll lead the way down the tables. Since you get to go first, you'll have first choice."

"I can't wait."

He led her up the couple of steps to a microphone standing on the deck. "Good afternoon. Thank you all for finding your way through the snow to help us celebrate today. The blizzard brought me the best present I could ever ask for. Isabella and Angel.''

His mother stepped forward and handed Angel to him. He took the baby in one arm, the other around Isabella. ''The two most beautiful females in the world. If you haven't met them, you will. They're going to be a fine addition to Rawhide.

''Now, Red and Mildred have been doing a lot of cooking, so I suggest you follow us to the buffet.'' They stopped by the baby bed they'd brought down for Angel. Once Russ had her tucked in, he took Isabella's hand and led her to the food.

Several hours later he stood leaning against the wall when Nick joined him. ''I can see Sarah is having a good time. We've got too many bachelors in Rawhide.''

''You're right about that. And I'm not into sharing when it comes to my wife,'' Nick grumbled.

''I know. Me, neither. You'll let me know when you talk to Izzy's dad? And what he says?''

''Of course. Hopefully we'll handle everything civilly. Tori says it's a strong company. She said Isabella could sell out and have a lot of money.''

''I know. I'm going to try to talk to her about that.''

''Good idea. Might be a good idea if the two of you went on a honeymoon now, after her dad learns he's lost controlling interest of the company. It would give him time to cool off.''

Russ looked at Isabella, doing a polka with one

of the ranch hands. ''I don't think she'd agree to go. Besides, running away doesn't sit well with me.''

''There are lots of Randalls available to fight for you.''

''I'm not a coward, Nick, but thanks for offering.''

The music ended and both men stepped forward to claim their women. Russ slid his arms around Isabella just as another cowboy stepped forward to claim her. ''Sorry, pal, but she belongs to me,'' he said with a smile, but his voice was firm.

''Yeah, lucky you.''

''You bet,'' Russ assured the man. Then he dropped a quick kiss on Isabella's lips and started moving to the waltz being played. ''Good thing you had a big meal. Otherwise you'd waste away with all the exercise,'' he teased Isabella.

''You're right. We have to go cut the wedding cake Mildred made. Have you seen it? It's beautiful.''

''How do you know we need to cut the cake?''

''Mom is signaling to me over your shoulder.''

Russ swung her around to see his mother waving to them. ''You're right.'' He stopped dancing and took her hand. ''Then, after we eat some cake, we can go home. Will you be ready?''

''Yes, I will. Those are wonderful words. I'll be ready to go home with my husband and child.''

''So will I, Mrs. Randall.''

Chapter Eleven

After the events of the past two weeks, the rest of the weekend was extraordinarily calm. Russ settled into one of the spare bedrooms in Isabella's new house. Together the two of them took care of Angel, shared the meals and the chores.

Russ trained himself to accept what he was given—Isabella's company and the presence of Angel. He wanted more, but he was going to have to work for it.

On Monday morning he offered to stay home with Isabella, but she assured him it wasn't necessary. She told him she was going to do some more sorting of Great-aunt Maria's belongings. And she asked him to bring home some groceries.

Russ went to the office, opened it and had settled down to work when Nick walked in.

''Russ? Got a minute?''

''Sure, Nick. Have a seat.'' He studied his cousin's face. ''It's about Isabella?''

''Yeah. Her father called first thing this morning

to ask when I would be sending Maria's belongings. I had to tell him that I'd been in contact with Isabella. He wanted to know where to find her."

"Did you tell him?"

"No. I told him that I would have her in my office tomorrow morning if he wanted to call and talk to the two of us together."

"I'll be there, too. What did you think of him?"

"I think he has a nasty temper."

"Did he ask about the shares?"

"Oh, yeah. He even threatened her via me. I told him it was illegal. He told me I shouldn't interfere between a man and his child."

"I will definitely come with Isabella tomorrow."

"Do you want me to call her or will you tell her?"

"I'll tell her. We'll have to arrange for a babysitter."

"Not necessary. Sarah would love to keep an eye on her upstairs while we take care of business. Would that work for Isabella?"

"Of course. And tell Sarah we appreciate it."

Russ sat for several minutes after Nick left before he reached for the phone. So much for the peace they'd enjoyed over the weekend.

"Izzy, Nick just came over. Your father called. He wanted to know where you were. Nick told him he'd have you at his office tomorrow if he wanted to call and talk to you."

"Oh. I guess I don't have a choice."

"You could put it off, but I think it would be better to get it over with. I'll come with you."

"But Angel—"

"Sarah volunteered to keep her upstairs while we take care of business."

"That's so nice of her. I met her sister, Jennifer, and the twins. Oh, and I met Nick's twin, Gabe. They seem very happy."

"Yes, they are. So tomorrow morning's okay with you?"

"Yes, of course."

"All right. I'm going to get to work. Oh, the garage called and your car is ready. Why don't I come pick you up for lunch? After we eat, I'll take you to the garage and you and Angel can take the car back home."

"You don't mind? Where would we eat?"

"The café across the street. The food's pretty good. I'll come get you at eleven-thirty."

"Okay."

Russ hung up the phone, but he had difficulty concentrating on his work. He didn't think Isabella was strong enough to deal with her father. They needed to talk with Nick to determine what she should say or do. It wasn't going to be easy.

ISABELLA WAS NERVOUS the next morning. She was glad Russ was going to be with her. He suggested they leave early to talk things over with Nick.

She needed to make some decisions. Was she willing to stand aside as her aunt had done? To be ignored, to take what he gave her? No, she wasn't. So what options did that leave her?

She wasn't sure.

At breakfast, Russ watched her.

"Why are you staring at me?" she asked.

"I'm worried how you feel about this morning."

"I hate it. I don't want to talk to him."

Russ reached across the small breakfast table and took her hand in his. "He's going to be difficult."

She gave a dry laugh. "I know. I've seen him in action. I need to decide what to do."

"Nick said the annual stockholders meeting is in a month. He'll have to have a decision before then."

"Yes."

When they got to Nick's office, Sarah was waiting to take Angel upstairs. But Tori was also waiting. Russ asked her why she was there.

"Nick thought I might be able to offer some suggestions to Isabella before the conversation. We both think she'll need to know what she wants to do before she talks to him."

"Well, I know I could give him power of attorney, like my aunt did, but I don't want to do that," Isabella said. "It seems wrong to reward a bully. What options do I have?"

"You could attend the stockholders meeting and unseat him. You would need to find someone to put in charge, someone powerful. If you left, your father could cause difficulties. He probably will even if you're there."

"Other options?"

"The best one, in my opinion, assuming you don't want to be involved in prolonged fights or to live in New York, is to start selling the stock, a little at a time so you don't flood the market and cause the price to drop, until it's all sold. Staying connected to this man or this company is sure to cause difficulties for you."

Nick added, "You would have plenty of money if you did that, and Tori can reinvest it for you."

Isabella stared at Nick and Tori without saying anything. Then she looked at Russ. "What do you think?"

"I like the last option. You wouldn't be intentionally trying to hurt your father, but you would remove a monopoly of power from his hands."

"Yes. All right, that's what I'll do. When can you begin, Tori? The sooner, the better."

"I can start—"

She stopped when the phone rang. Nick's secretary answered it. "Yes, Mr. Paloni. One moment, please."

Nick put the phone on speaker and said, "Good morning, Mr. Paloni."

"Mr. McMillan. Is my daughter there?"

"Yes, I'm here, Dad. My husband is here with me."

"Your what?"

"My husband, Russ Randall."

"Are you going to give me power of attorney?" he asked gruffly, ignoring Russ.

"No, I'm not."

"The stockholders meeting is in a month. I need it by then. What do you want for it?"

"I'm not going to give you power of attorney, Dad."

"You want to make me sweat? You know me better than that. You'll get hurt if you try to play that game with me."

Russ put a hand on Isabella's arm. "Mr. Paloni, I'm Russ Randall, Isabella's husband. Don't threaten her."

"This is between me and my daughter. Stay out of it."

"No, I won't."

"What? Is she offering you money? You hoping to cash in? Well, think again. I won't let that happen."

Nick leaned forward. "Mr. Paloni, you have no control over your daughter's decision. I'm sure she'll let you know her decision before thc meeting."

"She'll damn well let me know sooner than that or I'll—" Nick leaned forward and ended the call.

Russ put an arm around Isabella. "He can't hurt you, honey. He's a long way away."

"Of course." She looked at Tori. "How soon can you start selling off the stock?"

"Today. I don't think your father will expect such fast action. If he doesn't realize it's what you will do, he won't watch for it. So at least some of it will be bought by others before he can buy any of it.''

''Good. Please start at once. Will we be able to sell all of the shares in a month?''

''That shouldn't be a problem.''

Isabella felt a shiver run over her. She had a feeling there would be some problems.

THAT NIGHT AFTER DINNER, Russ asked Isabella to come into the den and sit down with him. She complied, but she was worried about what he wanted. If he started trying to seduce her, they'd have a fight. She wasn't ready yet.

She sat down beside him, but she left almost a foot between them. ''What is it, Russ?''

He grimaced, apparently recognizing her standoffishness. ''I want you to explain the problem between you and your father. He sounded absolutely vicious on the phone this morning. It bothered me.''

''It bothered me, too.'' She sat there, but she couldn't think what to say. It was only fair that he understand, but what if he wound up believing her father was right? Russ, and all the Randall men for that matter, seemed different from her father, but she wasn't sure she could trust her judgment.

''Isabella? I know it must be hard for you to talk about it, but...how else can I understand?''

''But what if you don't?'' she asked, upset that

her voice shook. She didn't want him to know how weak she was.

"You think I'm stupid?"

"It's not a question of stupidity. It's the way some men think."

"Tell me."

After a deep sigh, she began. "I told you my mother died when I was very small. I think I was about two. I only have faint memories of a beautiful woman who smelled good, who was gentle. After that, I only had my father. I adored him. He took me everywhere with him, sometimes even to the office. He taught me things about the business. At night, he read to me. Sometimes it was just the newspaper, but I didn't care because my daddy was sharing with me."

"So far, so good," Russ murmured.

"Yes. Then he met a woman he was attracted to. She took some of my time. I resented it, but I still was my father's pet, so I didn't protest too much. Then my stepmother got pregnant. She wasn't a bad woman. She let me feel the baby kick and talked about me having a playmate. When I turned ten, she threw me a birthday party. I overheard her tell my father it was important that I feel loved right now. I thought that was a funny thing to say. Of course I felt loved. My daddy loved me.

"Then the baby was born. A little boy. Suddenly Daddy didn't have time for me. He hung over the side of the crib. He carried the new baby around, talking to him. I never went anywhere with my daddy anymore. I begged him to take me with him, but he said women belonged at home, and I should spend time in the kitchen learning to cook. So I did. Anything to please my daddy. When I brought him a plate of misshapen cookies I'd made, he said he wasn't hungry. I pleaded with him. I'd made them for him. He wasn't interested.

"Things got worse, the older the baby grew. Soon he was going everywhere with Dad. I was left at home. I didn't understand. It seemed there was something wrong with me.

"I started sitting outside his office to pretend that he was including me. One night one of his friends asked about me because he hadn't seen me in a while. Daddy laughed. He said he didn't need me anymore. He had a son now. I was relegated to female things such as cooking and cleaning. He didn't have to pretend that he adored me. He said it was like when he was courting my stepmother. He had to pretend he loved her, couldn't get enough of her. Once he'd married her and got her pregnant, he didn't need her anymore.

"From that day on, I hated him. I tried to tell my stepmother what he'd said, but she refused to listen to me. I kept my distance from then on, but I tried to learn everything I could about business. I was determined to make my father pay for his words."

Russ scooted closer and put his arm around her. "Honey, your father is a stupid man. He gave up the sweetest things in life for his greed and his hunger for power. I don't blame you for hating him or for running away with Angel. You can have a dozen boys, but none of them would be Angel. Every child is precious, each with different talents. I would love them all.''

''I hope so.''

''You don't believe me?''

''I've learned it's best to wait and see. Besides, we won't have any boys. We won't have any babies at all because we're not going to...to, you know.''

''The words are 'to make love,' sweetheart. Did you love your last husband?''

''No. Once Daddy worked on him, I hated him for his weakness. He betrayed me as much as my father did.''

Russ pulled her chin around so she faced him. ''I will not betray your trust, Izzy. I promise.''

She wanted to believe him. She wanted so badly to believe him. She even wanted to make more babies with him. To lie in his arms and feel surrounded with safety and love. But she didn't have that kind of trust. ''We'll see.''

IT WAS ONLY a week until Christmas. So much had changed in the first three weeks of December that Isabella could hardly believe the holiday was approaching. She'd given up on Christmas along with everything else in her life years ago. But Janie insisted she go shopping with her. They took Angel with them and drove to Buffalo.

"Are the shops better in Buffalo?" Isabella asked.

"Some. Although the general store in Rawhide has some surprising things. And Megan's store, where some of Maria's things are for sale, has some nice things."

"Would Mildred be offended if I gave her and Red that painting she liked?"

"How sweet of you, Izzy. She'd be thrilled. I heard her telling Red about it. But I think the painter is famous now. You could probably get a lot of money for it."

Isabella rolled her eyes. "The money doesn't matter."

"You're such a wonderful person. Russ really got lucky."

"Mom, I took advantage of him."

Janie squeezed her hand and switched the topic back to shopping.

In the days following that shopping trip, Isabella visited the stores in Rawhide, looking for special presents. At night she wrapped the gifts and hid them. One day she bought a small tree and ornaments. That night she asked Russ to help her decorate it. She figured he'd refuse, but instead, he showed a real enthusiasm and talent for decorating.

"You like doing this?" she asked in disbelief.

"Sure. At the ranch, we don't do the tree until

Christmas Eve, but it seems a shame to me to wait so late. This way we'll get to enjoy it longer."

"We might not next year. Angel will be able to walk by then. She's liable to pull it over on top of her."

"We'll keep an eye on her. That will be fun, won't it?" He hung a blue ball on the tree. "I noticed you bought a lot of blue. I think you favor that color."

"Oh! I hadn't even noticed. I'm sorry."

"Don't bother apologizing. Since I met you, I'm a little partial to blue, also," he assured her, grinning.

She was embarrassed. She'd bought him a cashmere sweater as a present, and it was blue. Should she take it back and get a red one? No, she decided. She liked him in blue. She'd also bought him a new billfold. A beautiful handmade leather wallet made by a local Native American woman. She'd asked the clerk if the woman ever made little purses. The clerk promised to get a tiny one made with Angel carved on it the next day.

She'd also shopped at Megan's store and bought several gifts for the adults out at the ranch. A family the size of the Randalls required a lot of shopping, but it was fun. Isabella was finding it a pleasure to search for the right gift for Toby and Elizabeth, Rich and Samantha, Nick and Sarah, and Gabe and Jennifer. She was going to meet some other Randalls at Christmas. They even thought Caroline,

Toby's sister, might make it home for Christmas. And the ones in university would be home.

A real family Christmas.

Two days before Christmas, Janie called Isabella. "Hon, will you and Russ and the baby spend Christmas Eve night here? Everyone else will be here. We have enough bedrooms."

"Of course we'll come for the evening," Isabella replied, "but why do we need to spend the night?"

"Santa Claus comes in the morning. I'll admit it gets a little noisy, but it's also a lot of fun."

"I'll bet it is." Isabella thought of the stiff, formal Christmases she'd had, where money was spent on one gift, usually something "suitable," rather than something she wanted. The day had been dreary and sad for as long as she could remember. "Yes, we'll come!"

When she told Russ that evening, he wasn't as enthusiastic. "Are you sure? It's a bit overwhelming."

"I wouldn't miss it for the world."

He started to say something else, but then he simply nodded. "Okay, if that's what you want."

She found a recipe in one of her aunt's old recipe books for an Italian pastry. Christmas Eve morning, she spent hours making the pastry, a cannoli filled with vanilla cream. Then she made some with chocolate cream, since she thought everything chocolate was wonderful.

Russ had gone into town for a little while. When

he came back and saw the results of her cooking, he offered to be a taster. "We wouldn't want to take something that hadn't been taste-tested," he said, his eyes round with mock innocence.

She laughed, feeling especially happy today. "I think they're safe. But I'll let you have one after lunch. Then it'll be time to go to the ranch. Mom said to come as soon as we could."

"Uh, I explained to Mom that we didn't have time to shop, so don't feel embarrassed if we get presents. You've had too many things going on in your life."

"That's sweet of you, Russ, but I've done a little shopping," she told him. In reality, she was feeling a little guilty. The extra bedroom was so full of presents, you could hardly see the floor.

After lunch, she gathered all the things Angel would need. "These things need to go in the back of the truck," she said. "And while you're taking care of that, I'll bring down the gifts I've bought."

She piled a load of presents in the laundry basket. Then she brought it downstairs and turned it upside down on the rug by the door. Russ came in at the same time and stared in surprise.

"A little shopping, you said?" he asked, staring at her.

"Maybe I got a little carried away, but it was fun," she said, faintly embarrassed.

He started gathering the packages to take outside while she returned to the bedroom. It took four trips. Russ was laughing by the time he finished loading everything. ''Are you sure we're not moving in for a month?''

''I know it's a lot, Russ, but—''

''I'm not complaining, sweetheart. Just don't forget those cannolis you made. Everyone's going to call you Mrs. Claus. It's going to be a merry Christmas.''

She agreed.

Chapter Twelve

Isabella packed two large dishes of cannolis, one for the chocolate and one for the vanilla. She was shy about bringing anything to Red's kitchen, so she handed them to Mildred when they entered.

"What are these?" Mildred asked curiously.

"I wanted to contribute something to the festivities, so I made cannolis. They're Italian desserts."

Russ watched her, knowing she was nervous. But he'd tasted her contribution, so he wasn't worried. "Maybe you should try one, Mildred, so everyone will know they're all right."

"Right here in front of everyone?" Mildred asked. All conversation stopped and everyone stared at her.

Isabella said, "It's okay, Mildred. You don't have to."

"No, of course I will. Are there two different kinds?"

"Chocolate and vanilla, but you may not like the chocolate. The recipe only calls for vanilla, but I like chocolate.'' She reached out to take the large dish of chocolate ones.

''No, you don't, young lady. I'll try the chocolate ones. I feel the same way about chocolate.''

''So do I,'' Elizabeth said, reaching out for one herself.

''Now, don't you ruin your lunch,'' Red complained.

Elizabeth took her bite first. She closed her eyes as if in ecstasy. Then she said, ''What lunch?'' And took another bite.

Mildred nodded. ''You've got a point, Elizabeth.'' She turned to Isabella. ''Child, you are never to darken our door again—without a plate of... What are they called?''

''Cannolis,'' Isabella said with a sigh of relief.

Russ gave her a hug. ''I told you that you had nothing to worry about.''

''But Red is such a good cook.''

''I heard that!'' Red shouted. Then he smiled. ''And I like it!'' He selected one of the vanilla cannolis, took a bite and praised Isabella's effort.

Suddenly there was a rush, and half the cannolis were gone in no time. ''No more!'' Red ordered, and put the two plates on the kitchen cabinet where he could protect them. ''Lunch is ready. First call to the table.''

''First call?'' Isabella asked, looking at Russ. ''What's that mean?''

''Children. There are too many people to feed

everyone at once. So you eat according to your age.''

She laughed. ''I wondered how they would feed everyone. That makes sense.''

''Yeah. And since we've eaten lunch, why don't we unload the truck? I'll put Angel in one of those baby beds.''

''Any of them? Won't someone mind?''

''Nope. Those are kitchen beds for whoever needs one.''

When they came back in with their first load of gifts, some of the adults asked if there were more.

''Yeah,'' Russ said with a laugh. ''I married a shopaholic.''

''Russ! I am not. This is a big family.''

Everyone was laughing. ''We're not complaining,'' Toby said as he got up to help. ''We're hoping we might find something in here for us!''

''It's possible,'' Isabella said, raising an eyebrow, ''but no peeking.''

After the gifts were unloaded, Russ, with Rich's help, brought in their belongings for spending the night. ''Mom?'' he called. ''Where are we sleeping?'' He'd already realized there would be a problem. He was waiting for it to hit Isabella.

''This way, son. I'll show you. You're one of the lucky ones. You get a bedroom. Of course, most of your cousins are going to the bachelor pad.''

''The what?'' Isabella asked. She thought she'd already learned everything about the Randalls.

B.J. leaned over and said, ''It's a bunkhouse we

built for all the boys. They still take their meals with us, but it clears up a lot of bathroom lines and yelling and screaming.''

''I can imagine. That was a good idea.''

Her mind continued to think about the housing problem when everyone came home for Christmas. Then it hit her.

Bedroom. They would only get one bedroom. For the three of them.

One bedroom. One bed. Janie had opened a closed door and Isabella's eyes immediately confirmed her surmise.

''Sorry we're so crowded, Izzy. But it's just for one night. Is that all right?''

Isabella read the concern on Janie's face. She was afraid her new daughter-in-law was going to make a fuss. And Russ stared at her, too, his gaze calm and reassuring.

''It will be fine, Mom. Thanks for giving us a bedroom to ourselves.''

Janie kissed her on the cheek. ''There's a crib for Angel, too, so big old Russ won't roll over her.''

''Mom! I wouldn't.''

''In your sleep you might. Settle in and then come downstairs. Have you had lunch?''

''We have. My wife keeps me well fed.''

''Good. You could use a few more pounds.''

Isabella laughed at the outrage on Russ's face.

''This family is so much fun,'' she said when

Russ turned to protest. "Thank you so much for bringing me into it."

Janie kissed her cheek again. "We're the lucky ones, Izzy." Then she dashed out the door and down the stairs.

Quietly Russ said, "Thanks for not making a fuss about the one bed. Mom was worried about it."

"I know. I could tell. I can sleep on the floor or—"

"We'll both sleep in the bed, Izzy. I'm not a monster who can't control himself. It's a king-size bed, after all. There's plenty of room."

After looking at him for several seconds, she smiled and said, "Okay."

He relaxed and asked, "How's Angel? Think she'll sleep much longer?"

"Yes, I fed her right before we left. I think she'll sleep for hours."

"Want to go down and see how big a tree they got this year?"

"I didn't see a tree," she said as she opened her suitcase. She took out two baby monitors.

"It's hidden in the barn."

She stiffened. "With the horses?"

"Have I marked you for life with my tactics? I promise I won't put you on a horse, okay?"

"Thanks." She put one of the monitors in the baby bed beside the sleeping infant. She put the other one in her pocket. "There, we'll know if Angel wakes up early. I'm ready."

"You want to wear your mink coat? I put your

ski jacket in the closet downstairs after our last visit.''

''Oh. That was thoughtful of you. I forgot all about it. But it would be better for going to the barn.''

He gave her a quick hug, then stepped away. ''I just wanted to say thank you for trusting me again.''

She smiled and offered her hand. He took it in his and they headed for the barn.

''Where are you going?'' someone asked as they went through the kitchen.

''To see the tree.'' Russ's announcement got the attention of the college crowd and the little ones. Elizabeth and Toby's oldest, three-year-old Davy, immediately began shouting, ''The tree, the tree!''

His little sister didn't understand, but she knew she wanted to go if Davy did. Elizabeth's brother Jim took Davy, and Russ's brother Casey took one-year-old Steffie. The twins, Gabe and Jennifer's pair, were too young, two weeks younger than Angel, in fact.

''You know, in a couple of years we're going to have a herd of little ones,'' Red mused. ''I can't wait.''

Rich said, ''Ours is down for his nap, or he'd want to go now. And Jon and Tori aren't here yet with Jonny.''

''Then let's hurry before they get here,'' Russ said with a big grin. Everyone rushed out the door.

Isabella had put on her ski jacket. She followed

them out. Instead of leading the charge, Russ waited for her. "Warm enough?"

"Yes, this is a lovely jacket. I think I forgot to thank you. And the boots are nice, too, but I forgot to bring them."

"Your hat, too. But I don't think you'll need it for a walk to the barn, since it's not snowing."

"Does it snow often here?"

Russ laughed.

"What's funny?" Rich asked.

"My wife wanted to know if it snows often here."

"Oh, yeah," Jim said. "But school seldom closes. Just during the blizzards."

"I hadn't thought of that. In New York, while the snow is coming down hard, we stay home, but they get things opened up quickly with all the snowplows."

While they'd been talking, they'd reached the barn where the tree was stored. The adults threw open the barn door and everyone stood silent, staring at a majestic green tree leaning against the back wall.

"Will it fit?" Isabella whispered.

"I don't know. But the dads are pretty good at picking out the perfect tree. The living room has a raised ceiling," Russ added.

"It is beautiful. I've never seen such a big tree for a house. The one in New York's Rockefeller Plaza is huge, of course, but it's outside."

"We've seen that one on television. But I've always thought ours was more beautiful,'' Russ told her.

Isabella took a deep breath. ''It smells lovely.''

''It will smell even better inside. And after Christmas we hang oranges stuck with cloves and slices of apple smeared with peanut butter on the tree and put it outside so the birds can feed on it.''

''Oh! How perfect.''

He hugged her to his side and dropped a kiss on her cheek. ''That's us! The perfect Randalls!''

Rich leaned over. ''You won't think so at six in the morning.''

''What happens then?'' Isabella asked, puzzled.

''That's the earliest the kids can wake anyone up for Christmas.''

''S-six in the morning?'' She stared at Rich, and seeing the laughter in his eyes, she said, ''You're teasing me.''

Samantha shook her head. ''He's not. Santa brings each child one big present and they're not allowed to go downstairs until then. At seven, Red serves breakfast. Then about eight, we all go in and open gifts. That takes several hours, because we try to open one at a time, so everyone can see what everyone else got. It helps the parents, but it doesn't always work.''

Isabella was picturing the chaos Samantha was describing. ''I can't wait.''

Samantha grinned. ''Me, too. I'm as bad as the kids. I didn't know Christmas could be like this.''

''Me, neither,'' Isabella said softly.

She didn't feel quite so different from everyone else after that. Samantha had felt the same way she did. And Russ understood.

''Russ, can we go see the baby horses again? I bet the little ones would like to see them, too,'' she said, watching him.

''You sure you want to?''

''Yes. I'll get more used to them if I visit them. Samantha, were you afraid of the horses when you first came here?''

''No, Izzy. I started cleaning out stalls when I was five. I was used to horses.''

''She rides as good as me,'' Rich bragged, ''which comes in handy at roundup when I need everyone I can get.''

''You'll have me this year, bro,'' Russ said, his words a solemn promise. ''I won't leave all the work to you.'' Russ smiled at his brother.

Rich gave him a hug. ''Good.''

Isabella had never seen so much hugging between men. She liked it. ''I don't think I'll volunteer just yet. I have a lot to learn before I'll be of any use.''

''Make cannolis and I won't have any trouble getting volunteers. There's plenty for everyone to do.''

She smiled at Rich. ''You've got a deal. And thanks for making me feel welcome.''

After they visited the foaling barn, oohing and aahing over the gangly babies, they headed back to the house, only to meet the dads coming for the tree.

"Go clear a path through all those presents so we can get the tree in its place," Jake ordered. "Your moms are organizing the decorations."

Soon the entire family, except for the sleeping babies, were gathered in the living room. Everyone was given a decoration to hang on the tree. As soon as each person hung a decoration, he or she came back to the box and got a new one.

Isabella was surprised at how beautiful the tree looked in the end with so many people involved in decorating it. Then they moved the gifts to encircle the tree. The lights were plugged in and everyone fell silent. Then they began singing "Silent Night."

Tears formed in Isabella's eyes as she joined the singing. This life was what she wanted for Angel. What she wished she'd had. But now it was being given to her and her little girl. Thanks to Russ. She silently gave thanks for the blessings she'd received.

IT HAD BEEN a good day, Russ thought as he and Izzy climbed the stairs. After the tree was decorated and they'd done their traditional singing, they'd all made sandwiches. Red had made tomato soup to go with them. Then last-minute chores for the next day were tackled. Isabella suggested they make popcorn strings to go on the tree when they put it out for the birds, so everyone who didn't have something else to occupy their time worked on popcorn strings, and munched a few, too.

When the children were finally sent to bed, the parents started bringing out Santa gifts. Russ had watched Izzy as she'd talked to the other mothers and helped where she could. She fit in perfectly. He thought of Abby, remembering her enjoyment of Christmas. He'd been blessed twice.

Now it was almost midnight. Isabella was barely awake.

"I didn't know it would take so much energy for Christmas. Maybe you can take a few days off," she murmured.

"Maybe. I'll feed Angel tonight. You try to keep sleeping."

"I'll take you up on that, Russ. Thanks."

"We're sharing the bath with some of the others. But if you hurry, you can be first in line. I'll go down and make Angel's bottle."

When he got back to their room, Isabella was already in bed, sound asleep, her hair was loose and curling around her shoulders. He was glad he hadn't ruined things.

He decided he wouldn't go to sleep yet. The baby would be awake in another hour. Since Izzy had left the light on, he guessed it wouldn't bother her. He found a book left on the shelf and he started reading, sitting in the only chair in the room.

Angel slept longer than he expected. It was almost two o'clock when he heard her stirring. He greeted her with a whisper and offered the bottle he'd gotten ready. It didn't take her long to guzzle the contents. He figured she'd sleep until almost eight in the morning. Should he wake her mother to see the Santa presents? He wasn't sure he'd even get up.

He tucked the baby back into bed and was starting to undress when he heard a knock on the bedroom door.

Hurrying over to keep whoever it was from waking Isabella, he discovered his father waiting.

"Dad, what is it?"

"Come out here, son," Pete whispered.

He did as his father asked, fear building in his gut "Is something wrong?"

"The sheriff just called to be sure you and Izzy were here. Someone set your house on fire."

Russ's mouth fell open. Finally he asked, "Was it completely destroyed?"

"No. About half of it burned. We're going to drive to Buffalo because that's where the nearest hotel is and see if we can find whoever started it."

"You're sure it was arson?"

"Yeah. The sheriff is sure."

"Let me grab my boots." While he pulled them on, his anger grew. Isabella didn't deserve this. Who but her father would be responsible? Russ was ready to let him know how he felt about him.

He quietly left Isabella sleeping and went to join the men of his family.

Time to protect his loved ones.

Chapter Thirteen

Isabella came slowly awake the next morning. With Angel as an alarm clock, it had been a while since she'd awoken on her own. It was a real luxury. She finally raised her head to look for her baby and discovered the baby bed empty. Russ wasn't there, either.

He must be a quiet sleeper because she hadn't noticed him all night. She stretched and got out of bed. She'd brought a full skirt and a short sweater, one of her favorite outfits, to wear on Christmas day. When she thought to check the time, she realized it was almost eight-thirty. She'd missed breakfast and they must have already started opening the gifts.

She brushed her hair, leaving it loose, and hurried down the stairs. To her surprise, no one was in the living room and the gifts were all still in place. She headed to the kitchen, worry beginning to fill her.

''Morning, Izzy,'' Janie called. She sat at the

table feeding Angel. ‘‘Did you hear her cry? I tried to get her bottle ready as soon as I could.’’

‘‘No, Mom, I didn’t hear her. I’m sorry I...’’ As she started her apology, her gaze swept the kitchen and she realized Jake was the only man in sight. ‘‘Where is everyone?’’

The women all looked at Jake, so Isabella looked at him, too.

‘‘Izzy, someone set your house on fire last night.’’

‘‘What? Why would anyone— My father? My father set my house on fire? Oh, no,’’ she moaned. ‘‘No, surely he wouldn’t—he must’ve known we weren’t there.’’ She struggled to deal with what Jake had said. Then she put the missing men into the picture.

‘‘Where is Russ? And the others?’’

Jake shrugged. ‘‘They went with the sheriff.’’

‘‘Where? Where did they go with the sheriff?’’

‘‘To Buffalo. There are no motels in Rawhide, so any strangers would’ve had to stay in Buffalo,’’ Jake explained.

‘‘But...but it’s Christmas. We’ve ruined Christmas for all of you!’’

Janie held out a hand. ‘‘Come sit here with me, dear. We’re all safe. That’s the most important thing anytime, especially at Christmas. We’ll open the presents when they return.’’

Isabella felt as if she was sleepwalking. She wanted to shake her head and wake up to the happy world she'd shared last night. As soon as she sat down, Red put a mug of hot coffee in front of her.

"Drink it, girl. It'll help."

Still frowning, she managed to thank Red. "But what if they find...whoever did it?"

"I wouldn't worry about that," Jake said. "And you're safe here. I let the dogs out last night so we'd know if anyone came here."

"You mean I've put all of you in danger?" Isabella asked, horrified. She jumped up from the table. "Then I have to leave at once!"

"Nonsense," Jake said calmly.

"But you shouldn't have to suffer for me. I'll go pack," she insisted, starting for the door.

"Izzy!" Janie called out. "This is the safest place around. You're not going to put Angel in danger, are you?"

"Where would you go?" B.J. asked. "You don't have a home. And Russ will expect you to be here."

"But...but..."

"Honey, you're family—and we protect our own." Jake's voice was firm, sure.

Red slid a plate of waffles and bacon in front of her. "Whatever you do, you'll do better with food inside you."

She couldn't argue with Red's advice. She fell back into her seat and began eating. After a moment she asked, "You don't think the men are in danger, do you?"

"Nope. Besides, there's a lot of them."

They all stayed around the table in the kitchen, discussing past Christmases, telling funny stories to keep Isabella's spirits up. About noon, they received a phone call from Pete, telling them they'd be home in an hour and letting them know that everyone was all right.

"Thank goodness," Isabella breathed. Everyone was agreeing with her when Red called, "Car coming."

"Recognize it?" Jake asked, coming alert.

"Nope."

"Places," Jake snapped. "The rest of you stay here in the kitchen."

Isabella stared as Janie and B.J. grabbed rifles she hadn't even noticed standing in a corner. They slipped out the back door, grabbing coats as they went. Megan and Red headed for the stairs.

"What are they doing?" Isabella asked.

Jake had already headed for the front door, putting a pistol in the back of his jeans where it couldn't be seen.

"It's a better-safe-than-sorry plan," Samantha said. "Jake planned it earlier this morning."

"But we won't even know what's going on," Isabella protested.

"Jake said to stay here," Sarah said, "but if we're careful, I think a couple of us could go to the living room where we could hear what's going on. I'll go with you, Isabella, but we've got to stay out of sight, okay?"

Some of the women protested, but Mildred said

she thought it would be all right. But they were to come back and let the rest of them know what was happening every now and then. ‘‘And keep your noses out of sight!’’

Isabella kissed her baby goodbye. Then she and Sarah slipped down the shadowy hall into the living room. The two women got on their hands and knees and crawled to the front window.

Sarah whispered, ‘‘We’ll have to just listen.’’ She sat down on the floor and Isabella joined her.

They heard the car stop and one of the doors open.

Jake greeted the new arrival. ‘‘Howdy. Can I help you?’’

A voice that Isabella immediately recognized answered. ‘‘I’m looking for my daughter, Isabella Paloni, or Nick McMillan. Someone in town told me they would be out here.’’

‘‘They were. They’re not now. Want to leave a message?’’

‘‘I need to pick up some important papers. When will they be back?’’

‘‘I couldn’t tell you. They came over last night, but then they left. Haven’t seen them since then.’’

‘‘This is important.’’

‘‘Give me your name and if they come back, I’ll tell them.’’

‘‘I’m Antonio Paloni. My aunt died recently and I need to pick up her things.’’

‘‘What is your aunt’s name? Did she live here?’’

"Yes. Her name was Maria Paloni. You probably don't know her. She kept to herself."

"I knew her. Heard her house burned down last night."

"Really? I didn't know that. I assume no one was living in it?"

Jake shrugged his shoulders. "You've come a long way from New York."

"Actually I was in Chicago on business."

"I'll give Nick the message. He or your daughter will send you whatever is due you, I'm sure."

"Thanks, I appreciate that."

Isabella peeked out the window and saw her father's face through the window of his car as it backed up and headed back down the driveway.

Then, before she and Sarah could scoot back to the kitchen, Jake came through the front door. Isabella stood up, intending to apologize for disobeying him, but tears were streaming down her face. Jake pulled her to him and wrapped his arms around her. "You poor dear. He's not worth a plugged nickel. Did you want to talk to him?"

She shook her head no. Jake picked her up, carried her into the kitchen and set her down in a chair at the table. "Mildred, can you fix her a cup of chocolate? She needs something for shock."

B.J. and Janie came in from outside. They both hugged Isabella. "The man doesn't even care about you and Angel. He just wants the stock," Janie said.

"What happened?" several of them asked.

Jake gave a thumbnail sketch of what had happened, keeping it short for Isabella's sake. In the meantime, Red and Mildred got busy putting together Christmas dinner. Then all the women joined in except Isabella and Janie, who talked quietly.

"I thought he cared about me a little bit, but all he wants is the stock. I told him I was married and...he should've realized it would do him no good to come here."

"He's not thinking straight, honey. He probably thought you were lying to him."

"I don't know what to do."

Janie hugged her close. "Let's wait and see what the men have found out."

As if on cue, the sound of several trucks coming down the road reached their ears. "The men are back," Red announced.

Isabella grabbed her ski jacket and ran for the back door.

She flew into Russ's arms when he climbed out of the first truck, more tears rolling down her cheeks.

"Honey, what's wrong? Are you crying about the house? Don't worry. We'll build another one."

She shook her head, then buried it in his chest, not offering an explanation. Janie, who'd followed Izzy out of the house, gave Russ a brief synopsis of their day.

"Isabella's father came here?"

Jake, who'd followed the women out of the house, nodded. "Yeah, he was looking for Isabella or Nick. Nick!'' Jake called, waving him over. ''One of your clients came looking for you.''

''On Christmas Day? Who?''

''Antonio Paloni.''

Nick's eyes narrowed. ''What did he want?''

''He wanted you or Izzy to give him the papers for the stock. He still thinks he can talk you out of them.''

Russ's arms tightened around Isabella as she trembled against him. ''Damn it! Did you hear him, Izzy?''

She nodded again.

''Did it upset you, Izzy, that he only wanted the papers?'' Pete asked.

Isabella finally pulled back from Russ's embrace. ''I guess he went to the house, looking for the stock and was surprised to find it burnt down. When he couldn't find the company stock certificates, he came looking for Nick or me.''

''Russ, we need to talk.'' Isabella's gaze was pleading.

''Sure. Let's get inside out of the cold,'' he suggested. She turned and led the way. When they were inside, she headed upstairs, hoping he would follow. After stopping by Angel's bed in the kitchen and kissing her soft cheek, he did so. When they reached the bedroom they'd been assigned, she closed the door.

''I knew my father wanted the stock, but I didn't think he'd try to steal it. This is all such a mess.

He has a terrible temper. I don't want your family to have to see that. Maybe Angel and I should go."

He wrapped his arms around her. "No, Izzy. You promised to marry me and let me adopt Angel."

"Aren't you convinced that my father will stop at nothing to get what he wants?"

"Yeah, I'm convinced. But I don't give up easily. You're mine, you and Angel. Do you know how long it will take for Tori to sell those shares? Once she's done that, you'll have all the money you want for Angel, and your father won't be able to do anything."

"I don't know that I can avoid him for a month. And I don't want to bring trouble to your family."

"Our family. We're married. You belong to my family now. Do you know how much my mother loves you? My father?"

She pushed herself out of his arms. "They love me because you're alive again. But if I cause you anguish or harm, they won't love me. And I don't blame them. I'll hate myself."

"I'm not going to get hurt. We found the men who set the fire."

"What? How did you do that?"

"The motel operator took down their license plate. They came in from Chicago yesterday. They left the motel around two in the morning heading toward Rawhide. We caught up to them this morning. They'd just started back for Chicago. They had incriminating evidence in the trunk."

"But that doesn't mean my father was connected. Besides, he wouldn't have burned down the house without making sure the stock was safe.''

Russ smiled. ''We'll see. The sheriff hasn't had a chance to question the men yet.''

Isabella blinked back tears.

''It's going to be all right honey. Go wash your face. I'm going downstairs to talk to Tori. Then we'll have Christmas dinner.''

As they both started out the bedroom door, she caught a glimpse of his right hand. ''What did you do to your hand? Did you hurt it somehow?''

Russ looked at his hand and then hugged Isabella once more. ''I bumped it against something, that's all. I'll get Anna to clean it and put a bandage on it.''

''I can do that,'' she said, staring at his injured hand.

''We don't want to insult Anna. She's our official medical person. Hurry down, though. I'm starving.''

THE AMOUNT OF FOOD it took to feed the Randall clan was amazing. Instead of eating in shifts, as they usually did, extra tables were moved into the kitchen, along with chairs. When Isabella arrived in the kitchen, she found Russ's hand neatly bandaged. She looked at Anna.

''Thanks, Anna, for taking care of Russ. Was anyone else hurt?''

''If they were, they haven't complained. And Russ's hand will be fine tomorrow.'' Anna patted her gently on the back. ‘‘I think Russ saved you a place over there.’’ She pointed.

Isabella found her chair and sat. She was opposite Tori. ‘‘Did Russ ask how long it would take to sell all that stock?’’ she asked her.

‘‘Hey! It’s Christmas,’’ Russ complained.

Isabella was embarrassed. ‘‘Sorry,’’ she mumbled.

‘‘I can unload it quickly, but it will affect the price. Still, in the circumstances, the faster the better. What do you think?’’

‘‘I agree. Even if the price goes down, people are more important than money,’’ Isabella said.

Tori nodded. ‘‘Let me see what I can do. There was strong interest from one particular investor the other day. I might be able to make a deal if the buyer realizes you’re selling majority interest. The price might even go up.’’

‘‘Whatever you can do, Tori.’’

Nick and Sarah came to sit at their table.

‘‘Nick says I should apologize to you,’’ Sarah said.

‘‘For what?’’ Isabella asked, her eyebrows soaring.

‘‘For encouraging you to go to the living room to hear what was said,’’ Sarah said softly. ‘‘I know it was hard for you.’’

Isabella fought the tears that reappeared. ‘‘The truth is hard, but I had to know it.’’ She sniffed.

Red came over to the table to collect their plates,

which distracted everyone from Isabella. It gave her time to rein in her emotions.

"Jake is going to carve the first turkey. Your table is first. Line up and take your turkey. Then you can fill your plates at the kitchen counter. And leave some for the rest of us!" Red ordered.

Dinner was noisy but fun. The people at Isabella's table found a lot of interesting topics to discuss, which kept everyone away from the events of the morning.

When the telephone rang, Isabella was just forking up her last bite of stuffing. A silence fell over the room as everyone waited for Jake to answer the phone.

"Hello?"

Jake didn't indicate who was calling. He thanked the caller and promised to come into the sheriff's office in the morning. Then he sat back down as if nothing had happened.

Pete, sitting near him, asked a quiet question.

"Yeah," Jake said.

Russ protested. "Jake, tell us who that was."

"Better not. We'll talk later."

Isabella spoke clearly. "You might as well tell them, Jake. Everyone has sacrificed their Christmas for me. I can stand more news."

Jake looked at her consideringly. "I guess you're right, Izzy. In spite of your father, you come from strong stock." He drew a deep breath and said,

"That was the sheriff. The two men we caught confessed to setting the fire. But they wouldn't confess to anyone hiring them."

Isabella gave a sigh of relief.

Chapter Fourteen

Half an hour later the family had moved from the kitchen to the living room. Time to forget the earlier mess and open presents. Isabella was pleased that she'd done all the shopping she had. She'd received guidance from Samantha and Elizabeth, who'd encouraged her to search for special items, not necessarily expensive, but important to the recipient. It made opening the presents fun to watch.

When it was over, everyone began to pack up to go home. With no home to go to, Isabella stood in the living room, staring at the Christmas tree, trying not to cry. Strong arms slipped around her.

"Quit worrying," Russ whispered in her ear. "Your aunt's house was old and needed a lot of work. Now we can start over and build a good house for the future."

"But where will we live in the meantime?"

"Well, we have a choice. We can stay here or we can move back into my apartment. We'd have to share a bed, but we can do that and stick to the rules. And you'd be close to Sarah, Nick and Tori.''

Isabella turned in his arms so she could see his face. ''What do you want to do?''

''It doesn't matter, honey. It's only a short drive into town.'' He smiled, seemingly content with either choice.

''I'd like to live in the apartment if you don't mind. I don't want to hurt anyone's feelings, but—''

He stopped her by kissing her lips briefly and grinning at her. ''I agree. I'll explain it to my folks.''

''You might tell Red it's because he's too good a cook. I'll gain a ton of weight if we stay here.''

Russ laughed. ''Go pack your things. We'll borrow one of the baby beds until we can buy one at the store. And tomorrow you can replenish your wardrobe at Sarah's store. At least the beginnings of it. I bet she'll want to come help you.''

''Do you think she will?'' Isabella asked, her voice rising in enthusiasm.

''We'll ask her.''

The thought of buying new clothes lifted Isabella's spirits. Then she felt guilty for being so easily distracted from her real problems.

As if reading her mind, Russ whispered, ''Keep smiling, honey. It helps to keep your spirits up.''

''What are we going to do about those men?''

''We don't have to do anything. The sheriff has filed charges against them. I imagine the trial will be held in Buffalo, the county seat. It will take at least six months. We'll be in our new house by then.''

''We can build it before late spring?''

He took her by the hand and began pulling her in the direction of their bedroom so she could get ready to leave. ''We'll plan the house and hire the builder. Then he'll start as soon as we get a break in the weather. How many bedrooms do you want?''

That question distracted her. ''I guess four will be enough. After all, there are only three of us. That leaves us one bedroom for guests.''

''Hmm, we'll see.'' He waited until they were in their bedroom. Then he gave her a kiss on the lips again. ''Gather up everything and I'll go tell the folks.''

''Be sure you tell them how much I appreciate everything.''

''I will.''

RUSS'S PARENTS and other family members had as many questions as his wife.

''What are you going to do about her father?'' Pete asked.

Russ repeated what he'd told Isabella. Then he added the details about their new house.

''And we've decided to move back into the apartment until the house is ready. Izzy is afraid your feelings will be hurt, but I told her you'd understand.''

Janie smiled and squeezed her husband's hand to be sure he voiced no objections. ''That's fine with us,'' Pete agreed, ''but you're welcome here if you want to stay.''

''Izzy wants to start replacing things at once. It's handy when the store is just across the street.''

''We'll plan a trip into Casper when the weather gets better. Or we could even go to Denver,'' Janie suggested, her eyes lighting up at the thought.

Pete groaned. ''I'm going to have to work extra hard to pay for that.''

Everyone laughed because they all knew Pete could afford more shopping trips than Janie would ever make in her entire lifetime.

''Thanks to all of you for being so great, so supportive, for our first Christmas. Hopefully we won't cause such a stir next Christmas.'' He hugged his mother and his aunts, then shook all the men's hands. Then he hurried up the stairs to help Isabella with the bags and Angel.

Meanwhile downstairs, Pete whispered to Janie, ''Why did you squeeze my hand?''

''Because I think it's a good idea for them to stay in the apartment.''

''Why?''

She smiled. ''Because they'll only have one bed.''

THE APARTMENT HAD BEEN sitting empty for two weeks, so the newlyweds had some housecleaning to do. It was chilly there, too, because Russ had turned the furnace down, just keeping it warm enough to prevent the pipes from freezing.

Isabella discovered that Russ had taken the sheets he used to the house in case they needed them. "We have no sheets!" she exclaimed after looking in the hall closet for them.

"Nope. I should've brought some from the ranch, but I didn't think of it. Want me to drive back out there?"

It was already getting dark and Isabella was tired after the difficult day. "No, of course not. We can manage without sheets. I'll buy us some more tomorrow."

"Okay. I didn't take much out of the kitchen when we moved except...damn, I took the coffeepot."

Isabella dug into the pantry. "The jar of instant coffee is still here."

"Okay. That will do for a day or two. Good thing we brought our supper with us." Red had insisted on packing them some leftovers.

"Yes, because there's not much in the pantry." Isabella began arranging what was there. Then she suggested they eat first. Since Angel would probably wake up around six or seven, Russ agreed.

"I'm glad I left the television here. Your aunt had a pretty good television, but it was ruined in the fire. But at least we have one. There are some basketball games on tonight."

Isabella shook her head.

"What? You don't like basketball?"

"I like it fine. It just seems strange to sit and watch men playing with a ball when our lives have changed so dramatically. Three weeks ago, I wasn't sure I'd survive the storm. A lot has happened in three weeks."

"Yeah. I'm married." He put his hands on his hips almost as if to challenge her.

"Well, so am I!"

On that note, they sat down at the small table and ate the delicious leftovers. Red had even cut sizeable pieces from several cakes for dessert.

Angel awoke right on schedule. "I'll feed her while you put the baby bed together. Can we get it into the other bedroom without dismantling anything?" Isabella asked.

"Sure. I'll have it ready in no time."

When he came out of the second bedroom, Angel was sitting in her mother's lap cooing at her.

"Hey! She's talking!" Russ said. "Can she say anything?"

"Not unless you count 'googoodada' as anything," Isabella said with a laugh.

Russ grinned. "She's a joy, isn't she?"

"Yes. Dad can have the stupid stocks if it means Angel is safe," Isabella said vehemently, hugging her baby close.

"Right. But I don't think we have to worry about him anymore."

"I hope not."

She carried the baby into the other room and laid her down in the baby bed. Then she tucked the cover around her. The furnace was doing a good job of warming the place, but there was still a slight chill in the air.

Angel squirmed a little. Then her eyes fluttered closed and her even breathing indicated she was asleep.

"I guess she'll sleep until one or two now. I like having her sleep six hours between feedings," Isabella said.

"Yeah. 'Cause I can't go that long without eating."

"Go turn on the basketball game and I'll cut our pieces of cake," Isabella told him. They'd decided to have their dessert later.

"Good. I was hoping you'd take the hint." He settled on the sofa, but he soon realized they'd need a blanket to keep warm. He pulled one from the hall closet and spread it over himself, leaving plenty of room for Isabella.

Soon they were both snuggled under the blanket, their body warmth keeping each other warm. Isabella ate her cake, but she didn't have much interest in basketball. Soon she put her head on Russ's shoulder and fell asleep. It had been a long day.

Russ settled back in the corner of the sofa and drew Isabella between his legs, her back to his chest, and wrapped his arms around her. He was more content than he'd been in a long time.

They both slept until Angel woke up at almost two o'clock.

"I'll get her," Isabella mumbled, still half-asleep.

"I'll fix the bottle," Russ called after her, thinking how content he'd been with Isabella in his arms, how good it had felt. How right. He thought he'd never love again. But Isabella was changing his mind. The thought scared him, but he already knew she was an important part of his life. He loved Isabella.

When Isabella came back to the living room, Angel in her arms, Russ was waiting with the bottle, having warmed it in the microwave. He settled on the sofa again and wrapped the blanket around all three of them.

"I didn't intend to spend the night on the sofa," she said. Then she gave a gigantic yawn.

"Don't do that. You'll start me yawning."

"Who won the basketball game? Your team?"

"I don't know," he said. "I guess I fell asleep before it ended."

She chuckled, which caused the baby to fuss. "Behave yourself, Angel."

"She is, Mommy. She's perfect."

Isabella chuckled again, a sound Russ loved. "I'm going to have to keep an eye on you or you'll spoil her."

"Yeah. But that's what daddies are for."

Which unfortunately reminded Isabella that her father couldn't be included in that group.

Russ put his arm around her. "Don't think about him."

"You're right. I won't."

When Angel had been burped, Russ offered to carry her to her bed.

"Okay. I'll see what I can do with our bed." Those last two words struck her as extremely intimate. Nonsense, she told herself. They were sharing a bed, but that was all.

She spread a soft blanket on the mattress, then added several more for covers. She put the two king-size pillows each in its place, leaving space between them.

Russ came in as she finished. "That looks good. I got some flannel pajamas for Christmas. Why don't you take the top and I'll take the bottoms?"

Without waiting for her agreement, he tossed the long top to her and went into the bathroom. She stared at the blue top. It would come to her knees. Okay, she'd wear it tonight. The nightgown she'd worn at the ranch needed to be washed.

Russ opened the door and came out, his chest bare. "You're turn."

"You need to find a T-shirt. You shouldn't sleep with your chest bare in this weather. You'll catch a chill." She hurried past him, not waiting for his agreement.

After she'd disappeared, he rummaged in a drawer and found a T-shirt. He pulled it over his head. He had no intention of telling her to add clothes, however. He figured he could keep her warm. Not what he should be thinking. But he'd enjoyed their time on the sofa.

When Isabella came out of the bathroom, he was already under the covers, facing away from her. She turned out the light and slowly approached the bed, having misgivings now. They hadn't actually shared a bed last night, as she'd initially thought. He'd never made it to bed. She lifted the covers and waited, but he didn't move. Could he already be asleep?

She got in bed with as little disruption as possible. She felt the heat of his body, as she had on the sofa. He stayed in place and she turned her back to him and settled in. She was ready for some sleep.

It didn't take long for the softness of the bed and the warmth to tempt her to relax and sink back into sleep. Just as she was losing consciousness, she felt Russ move. Next thing she knew, he was drawing her against him, his arms circling her. She was going to protest, but she forgot why. She was way too comfortable to do so.

WHEN HE AWOKE early the next morning, Russ didn't move at first. He was too comfortable. Isabella smelled good and warmed him from his head to his toes.

About the only thing that could lure him out of bed would be a pot of coffee, but he remembered they only had instant. He'd take Izzy and Angel to the café for breakfast. He liked showing off his little family. That would give them a good start to the day.

He slid out of bed and took a shower. He pulled

on old jeans and a flannel shirt he'd gotten for Christmas. It was only eight o'clock. Did he dare wake Isabella? She could use the extra sleep. Then he remembered she'd been asleep by eight the night before. Twelve hours should be enough.

He sat down on her side of the bed as he pulled on clean socks. "Izzy?" he said softly. "I'm going to the café for breakfast. Why don't you and Angel come, too?"

She opened one eye in surprise. Then she closed it again. He waited and sure enough, the eye popped open again, wider this time. "What time is it?"

"It's a little after eight. But that's almost twelve hours of sleep you've had. Are you still tired?"

"No," she said slowly, drawing out the one syllable. "I don't think so."

"Will we wake Angel if we take her with us?"

"I hope not, because I refuse to leave her here alone," Isabella said, but she was smiling.

"Good. Want a shower before we go? I can wait that long if you hurry."

She pushed back the covers, laughing, until she realized the pajama top wasn't around her thighs but had climbed to her waist, leaving her pink panties visible. She yanked the covers back up. "Why don't you go make a bottle for Angel just in case she wakes up? We want to be prepared."

"Yes, ma'am," he drawled, and left the room, a big grin on his face. He fixed the bottle and waited. Then he decided to change Angel's diaper. She fussed a little, but he got her back to sleep.

By then, Isabella reappeared in the skirt and blouse she'd worn the day before. Her hair was pulled back with a matching scarf tied around it, but a few curls escaped. She looked wonderful.

"You look great, Izzy. And I'm starving. Let's go."

"I think I should change Angel now."

"I just did. She's gone back to sleep like a good girl. I put the bottle in the diaper bag and some extra diapers. Okay?"

"Definitely okay. You make a wonderful mom."

"Dad. I'm the dad, remember?" he teased.

"I remember. I was very lucky to run across you in that snowstorm."

"I think we were both lucky. What are you going to order for breakfast?"

"What do they do best?"

"Their pancakes are hard to beat. The cinnamon buns are famous. And they make great omelettes. The Denver omelette is their specialty. Casey, my little brother, loves their French toast."

"My, they have a wide menu."

"They need one. They're the only place in town for breakfast," he said.

They were glad to get out of the bitter cold and into the café. "I don't remember it being that cold last night," Isabella said. She breathed the warm fragrant air inside.

"It wasn't. Must have been a temperature drop overnight." He nodded to the waitress who then showed them to a booth. Isabella slid in the far side and reached for the baby in her carrier, which Russ had brought in.

"Let's put her over here," Russ suggested. "This carrier takes up a lot of space. I'll sit with you."

Isabella started to protest, but Russ was already seated.

"That way we can talk without disturbing Angel, too," he said.

The waitress handed them menus and turned away to escort another couple, who'd just entered, to seats.

"Oh, look, it's Sarah and Nick." Isabella waved to them and the pair approached.

"We were going to ask to join you, but I see Angel has this side full," Nick said, nodding to them.

"We can pull up a chair and put her carrier in it," Isabella said. "Then you can sit across from us. We'd love to have you join us."

"Did you go back to the apartment?" Sarah asked as Nick fetched another chair. "We saw lights last night and hoped it was you and not some mischief maker."

Nick moved the carrier and Isabella didn't answer until she was assured her baby was settled. "Yes. It's not too crowded. But we don't have any groceries yet. I'll have to do some grocery shopping today, among shopping for other things."

"Me, too," Sarah said. "I'm looking forward to

our shopping today. Will you be ready to start when we've finished breakfast?''

''Won't it be too early for the stores to be open?'' Isabella asked, looking at her watch.

''That's the joy of shopping with the owner. *I* have a key.''

''We can do that?'' Isabella asked, surprised laughter in her voice.

''You bet we can.''

Breakfast was thoroughly enjoyable. Isabella forgot the reason she needed to buy more clothes or why they were in the cramped apartment. She and Sarah talked about pregnancy and Jennifer's experience with twins. The guys joined in occasionally and had other conversation at times.

''What a nice way to start the day,'' Isabella exclaimed when they'd finished.

''It was, wasn't it? And we don't have to do the dishes,'' Sarah added with a big grin.

''And now we get to shop all day. Maybe I should wake Angel and give her her bottle now,'' Isabella debated, a frown on her face.

Russ leaned over and kissed her on the lips. ''Nope. I'm taking Angel until after lunch. When she wakes up, I'll feed her and put her back to bed.''

''But you said you have to work.''

''I do, but Angel can come to work with me. Bill's a grandfather, Tori's a mother. They won't be shocked.''

''Are you sure, Russ? I mean, I can take her with

me. She's not that much trouble, though it would be nice..."

"I'm sure. You two go ahead and scoot out. Nick and I'll have another coffee before we pay the bill."

Nick smiled, but his brow was furrowed. "Before you go, I have to bring up one unpleasant thing, Izzy. I had a call from your father. He wanted to know about your great-aunt's estate. I told him everything went to you."

"And he wasn't overjoyed, I'm sure," she said dryly.

Nick shook his head. "He told me you should forward to him the power of attorney for voting the stock right away. I told him I'd talk to you."

"I'm not giving him the power of attorney, as you know. Thanks for talking to him, Nick. It's more than I want to do. Ready, Sarah?" Isabella asked as she motioned for Russ to let her out of the booth. The two women hurried out the café, ready to start their shopping.

Nick waited until the door closed behind them before he spoke. "I think we should discuss some problems before I broach them to Isabella."

"Sure," Russ said, nodding expectantly. "What do we have to look forward to?"

Chapter Fifteen

"It's not that bad," Nick said, "but the sheriff called me this morning. He called the New York Police Department this morning to find out if Paloni has a record. He got no help from them since he has no hard evidence on Paloni."

"I want to talk to Tori about unloading that stock as quickly as possible. I don't want Izzy connected to her father at all." Russ sighed and rubbed his forehead.

"I'll walk over to the office with you," Nick said, "if Tori is coming in this morning."

"I think she is. Maybe she'll be willing to keep an eye on Angel while I run over to the sheriff's office, too."

"Good plan." Nick nodded. "I'm going to have to get used to making room in our lives for a baby. What's it like?"

Russ looked at Angel, sleeping in her carrier. "It's wonderful. Angel is such a good baby."

Nick chuckled. "You've sold me, Russ. And I'm happy for you."

Russ was embarrassed, because he knew Nick was referring to his change of behavior. "I let my mourning take control of my life. Thanks to Angel and Isabella, I've recovered."

"I know. Your mom's face shows it."

"Yeah," Russ agreed with a grin.

The two men picked up Angel, paid their bill and walked over to the accounting office.

"Bill!" Russ exclaimed when he discovered the older man hard at work. "I told you you didn't have to come back this week. After New Year's is soon enough."

"Morning, Nick, Russ. I know, but my wife went to work today. And you know I love my work."

Russ smiled. "You saved my bacon the last two years, Bill. I know Tori gave you your Christmas bonus. But I have your New Year's bonus in my office. I'll get it."

He excused himself and went into his office with Angel, returning a moment later with an envelope, which he handed to Bill.

"Russ, you don't need to—"

"Yes, I do, Bill. You've been an incredible asset to us. I want you to know I appreciate it." He deliberately changed the subject. "Has Tori come in?"

"She called about half an hour ago and said she'd be coming in for a while." As he looked at his watch, the door opened and Tori entered. "A welcoming committee? Really, it isn't necessary,'' she teased the three men.

They all laughed.

Tori asked, ''What's up?''

''I need you to watch Angel for a few minutes while I visit the sheriff,'' Russ said.

''No problem.''

''And can you tell me how the sale of that stock is going?'' he asked. ''I want Isabella's father to know that Isabella has nothing to do with him or his company as soon as possible.''

''Me, too,'' Nick added.

''Let me turn on my computer and I can tell you right away. I had a question about how much stock I had to sell. I should have a response by now.''

Leaving Angel with Bill, Nick and Russ followed her into her office. ''Of course, it could be that everyone isn't back at work, but we'll see,'' she said as she slid into her chair and turned on the computer.

Nick and Russ sat quietly as she played the keys like a concert pianist. ''Here it is,'' she muttered.

Russ felt tense, but a sound from Angel made him forget the other problems. He leaped to his feet and ran for his office. He found Bill already there, checking to see if she was all right.

''Thanks, Bill. She probably needs a change. I don't think it's feeding time yet.''

''Then I'll let you take over. Grandpas don't have to do diaper duty. Tori told me.''

Russ grinned. "Don't mention that rule to Dad, okay?"

Bill laughed and retreated to his desk.

"Okay, Angel, I'm going to change your diaper now, so be a little lady, okay?" he asked. He was sure she smiled at him, but he didn't know if that meant "yes" or "watch out."

Once he had her changed, he carried her into Tori's office. "Angel is joining us."

"Good." Tori said. "I want to hold her." She held open her arms.

Russ gave Angel to her as he asked, "Did you find a response?"

"Yes. It gets a little complicated and I won't do anything until I talk to Isabella, but there's a company that wants to take over her father's company. They'll pay five dollars a share above market price if she'll sell to them exclusively. Then they'll do a hostile takeover. It means her father will lose his position. While most employees will keep their positions, he's not one of them."

"I wish I could tell you what Isabella will decide, but I can't. I know she's angry with her father, but...I have a fear that she'll change her mind and go back to New York."

"But you're married!" Nick protested.

Russ regretted having admitted his fear. He'd worried about it, but he hadn't told anyone. Now he'd told both Tori and Nick. He looked at Tori. Her eyes were serious as she said, "I think I should call her. Are she and Sarah shopping?"

"Yeah. If you'll watch Angel, I'll run over there and find them. It won't take a minute."

"Sure thing," Tori said.

"I'll go with you," Nick said. "I miss Sarah."

Tori laughed at what she considered his silliness, but Russ knew what he meant. He hated being without Isabella and Angel, too.

SARAH CALLED through the closed curtains, "I found a blue sweater that would go well with the denim jumper, Izzy. Want to try it?"

Isabella stepped out from behind the curtain, wearing a plaid flannel shirt with the jumper. "I like this combination. What do you think?"

"Oh, it looks good."

"I love the big pockets. I can use my hands for Angel but carry other things in my pockets. And it's so comfortable."

"You're right. And then you change the shirt and it looks like a new outfit."

"Good point. Show me the sweater." Sarah held up the sweater, a thin silk.

"Ooh, very nice."

"Yes. Did you want a denim skirt? It goes with all the blouses and tops you've put aside."

"Yes. A size ten. I don't think I need to try it on."

"Probably not. Oh, I bet you need socks. I'll go— Oh! There's Nick and Russ. I think they're coming in."

''Maybe Angel is causing problems,'' Isabella guessed, and started toward them.

The men called a greeting and Russ noted Isabella's anxious expression.

''Nothing's wrong Izzy. Tori has a question for you, and she needs an answer right away. I thought you wouldn't mind interrupting your shopping to step over to the office.''

''Of course. Where's Angel?''

He wrapped his arms around her, unable to resist. ''She's perfectly safe in Tori's arms.''

''I know I shouldn't worry, but—''

''It's your nature.'' He looked down at her as she stepped away. ''I like that outfit. Are you buying it?''

''Yes. I like it, too.''

''Keep it on. You can show Tori.''

''Is that okay, Sarah? I mean, I haven't paid for it yet.''

''Yeah, but I know where you live,'' Sarah said with a grin.

Isabella smiled back. What fun to shop with Sarah! What fun to actually have a friend. Her father had tried to keep her from making friends.

''Here are some navy knee socks to wear under the long jumper,'' Sarah said. ''They'll keep your legs warm.''

Isabella took the socks and pulled them on. Then she slipped on her loafers. Those and her boots were the only shoes she had.

''Okay, Russ. I'm ready.''

He took her hand, knowing she wouldn't fuss about that. Besides, he liked holding her hand. "I'll bring her back in a few minutes, Sarah."

"I'll be here. Though Nick probably won't. He should go to work since it's after ten o'clock, right, lazybones?"

Nick didn't answer because he was busy kissing his pregnant wife.

Isabella slipped into her ski jacket and stepped outside with Russ. A north wind caused snow to swirl about them.

Izzy shivered. "It's still so cold," she said. Russ put his arm around her shoulders, pulling her close. "It'll warm up by June," he said.

She made her fist and hit him in the chest. "That was mean."

He kissed her in the middle of Main Street. Her cheeks fired up and she pulled away. "We could've gotten run over. That was dangerous."

"Yeah, 'cause there's such heavy traffic today."

"Okay, you have a point," she said, smiling as she stepped on to the sidewalk in front of the office.

When they were inside, Tori praised Angel and admired Isabella's new outfit, then got down to business.

Russ asked, "Do you want me to stay or leave the two of you alone?"

"I want you to stay, of course," Isabella said, surprised by his question.

He was gratified and sat down beside her.

"Okay, Tori, what do you have to ask me?"

Tori explained the offer for the stock and that the competitor wanted to do a hostile takeover of Paloni Industries. "Your father will lose control of his company and probably his job," she finished. "I couldn't agree to all that without getting your approval."

Isabella drew a deep breath. "Thank you. I don't want to be cruel to my father, but he would still have his money, wouldn't he?"

"He could sell his shares for a great deal of money, probably more than they are worth right now. I don't know what else he has, but he would keep any other holdings."

Izzy thought of her father's many investments. She knew he had spread his money around. In the past, whenever she'd asked for something expensive, he'd always claim poverty, but she knew better. If nothing else, they'd have her stepmother's jewelry collection.

"If he'd left me an option, I might have refused to do that to him, but I can't be a part of the company, so I have to sell. He would advise me to take the highest price without worrying about anyone else. As long as it wasn't him. So, yes, Tori, do the deal."

"Are you sure, honey?" Russ asked.

"Don't you think it's the right decision?"

"Yes, I do, but I want you to be sure."

"I'm sure. Tori, when will this take place?"

"Well, it's just a little after noon in New York, but I should be able to get hold of the buyer sometime this afternoon. By tomorrow morning, word should get to your father.''

Isabella wasn't a coward. She stood. ''I have to go to New York tonight.'' She was going to look her father in the eye and tell him what she'd done. And why.

''What?'' Russ gasped, leaping from his chair to take her arm, as if he was afraid she'd take off at once.

''I intend to face him with what I've done. And tell him my reasons, in case he hasn't figured them out. Will you take care of Angel? I don't want to put her at risk.''

''No, I won't,'' Russ returned, shocking her.

''But—''

''My parents will care for Angel. I'm going with you.''

''Why would you do that? I won't take the time to play tourist. I'll only be gone two days.'' It would be a difficult two days. She didn't want Russ to see how awful her family could be.

''You're not going unless I'm with you, sweetheart. I'm not letting you put yourself in danger.''

''Why would he hurt me after the deed is done?'' Isabella asked.

''A man's pride can be a fierce thing. Believe me, there is that possibility. Angel needs you to come home safely, and it's my job as your husband to make that happen.''

''But I wouldn't ask you to put yourself at risk, Russ. That wouldn't be fair.''

"I don't believe you did ask me. But ask or not, I'm going with you."

Tori interrupted their argument. "I believe there's a five-o'clock flight out of Casper that connects in Denver to the red-eye to New York. Shall I make reservations for you? I think you can make that one."

"Great," Russ said. "And get us reservations at some hotel in Manhattan. We'll hire a car for in the morning."

"But, Russ..." Isabella couldn't voice her protest. The idea of having him beside her was too tempting.

He kissed her again, something he did frequently these days. "We're either both going or neither of us is going. Your choice."

"I have to face him," she muttered.

"Then go pack a bag."

"First I have to buy one," she said. "Should I buy you one, too?"

"No, I've got a hanging bag in the apartment upstairs. Good thing I didn't move all my stuff into the house yet." He checked his watch. "It's a two-hour drive to Casper. We should leave by one-thirty. I'll meet you back here. Kiss Angel goodbye. I'm taking her to the ranch."

"Kiss her goodbye now? But...but we're not leaving for three more hours," Izzy complained, going to Tori for her daughter.

"You've got a lot to do before we leave. It will be easier this way."

Isabella reluctantly agreed. She cuddled Angel for a moment. Then she kissed her chubby little cheeks several times and held her against her. Giving her to Russ was hard. But even though she had tears in her eyes, she smiled. She wasn't going to leave her baby looking unhappy. She wanted Angel to remember her as happy.

Russ took the baby into his office and settled her in her carrier. Then he wrapped the heavy blanket over her to protect her from the cold.

"Aren't you going to call them first?"

"No, honey, I'm not. They'll agree to take care of her. And everyone in the house is capable of doing that. She's going to be just fine. Go buy what you need."

He picked up the carrier and went past Izzy as if he were merely delivering the mail. She followed him to the door. Again he kissed her on the lips. Then he headed for his truck. Isabella sighed. Russ was such a wonderful man. She didn't deserve the care he gave her, but she wanted it. She wanted more. She wanted a long life, beside him, wrapped in his arms and in his love. She gave a silent prayer. Then, she soberly returned to the store, a different list forming in her mind.

At night, during the week, the town of Rawhide rolled up the sidewalks a little after nine, when the café closed its doors. So at ten-thirty that night, no one was on the street when a black Cadillac drove into town.

The car stopped in front of the sheriff's office. It

made a U-turn and parked facing the way it had come in. On the road to Buffalo. The man who got out was distinguished looking, wearing an expensive suit, carrying a lawyer's case. He climbed the steps to the office and opened the door, stepping inside.

The deputy on duty had his feet propped up on the desk, watching a television. His feet came down in a hurry and he stood. "May I help you?"

"I'm here to see the two prisoners you have for setting a fire. I'm their lawyer from Chicago."

"Well, they've gone to bed. Why don't you come back in the morning."

"Young man, I have appointments in the morning. I must see them tonight. They won't mind losing sleep for me."

"Well, I guess it's okay." He opened the locked door to the jail area and then went back to watching television.

A few minutes later, the lawyer came back through the door. The deputy never even looked at him. The gun with the silencer came up and he fired. Then he left the sheriff's office followed by the two men the sheriff had arrested. The three men climbed into the Cadillac, no hurry or alarm in their motions. The Cadillac quietly drove out of town.

Chapter Sixteen

It was three a.m. in New York when Russ and Isabella arrived at the hotel in Manhattan. Isabella had fallen asleep on his shoulder in the taxi and he gently awakened her.

"Sweetheart, we're at the hotel. Come on. You'll be in bed soon."

At the check-in desk, the night clerk welcomed them and efficiently handed them a key. "Oh, there's a message for you, Mr. Randall," he said as Russ was about to turn away.

Isabella, having leaned sleepily against Russ, straightened immediately. "Angel? Is something wrong with Angel?"

Russ unfolded the note, apprehension in him, too. "No, sweetheart. It's from Dad. He thought it would make you feel better if you knew Angel is doing fine." He put the folded note in his coat pocket and led his wife to the elevator.

Half an hour later, when Isabella was again asleep, Russ slipped from the room and went downstairs to the bank of phones off the lobby. His dad answered the phone on the first ring.

"It's Russ. What's wrong?"

"I didn't want to tell you, but I thought you should know before you faced Isabella's father," Pete said hurriedly. "The two witnesses escaped. A man who claimed to be their lawyer came into the jail about 10:30 last night. The deputy didn't even search him," Pete pointed out in disgust. "He went into the cell area and released the men. Then he came out and shot the deputy, who was watching television."

"Who was it?"

"Jack Hayes. He didn't die, though he's injured. He managed to dial the sheriff's number after the phone fell to the floor. Otherwise, he would've bled to death."

"I intend to go straight to the airport from Isabella's father's office. I understand Isabella's wanting to face him, but I don't like the idea."

"I know. A few of us should have gone with you."

"Don't worry, Dad. I'll take care of her. I don't think I'll tell her until we're on the plane coming home." Russ hadn't made up his mind until that moment.

"All right. Take care, and give us a call when the plane has taken off."

"Will do. Thanks for the warning."

Russ hung up the phone and returned to the elevator. He had some thinking to do. Isabella had wanted to warn her father of her appearance at his company, but Russ had talked her out of the warning. Russ still liked the idea of surprising Paloni.

He entered their room and stared down at Isabella's peaceful, beautiful face. How could anyone be so mean to her? He changed and got in bed beside her, pulling her into his arms. It was getting difficult for him to sleep without holding Isabella. And tonight he needed what sleep he could get.

Russ forced himself out of bed at nine. He took his shower and dressed before he woke Isabella.

"Time to get up, honey. It's nine-thirty. We need to catch a taxi by ten o'clock."

She opened her eyes and sat up, staring at him.

"Do you remember where we are?"

"Of course I do, but...but you're dressed like a...a businessman."

Russ looked down at his white dress shirt, maroon tie and gray suit. "I *am* a businessman."

She scrambled to her knees and peered over the side of the bed to see his shoes, polished black wing tips. "Where are your boots?"

"In the suitcase. I think you'd better hurry if we're going to keep to our schedule."

She gasped at that reminder and hurried to the bathroom. He sat down on the bed, a grin on his face, and called room service. Their breakfast arrived fifteen minutes later.

Isabella emerged from the bathroom in the simple navy suit and shoes Sarah had provided. "Very nice,'' Russ told her with a smile. ''No one would guess you'd had a baby two months ago.''

Izzy blushed, but smiled and thanked him. They ate a quick breakfast and hurried outside to claim one of the many taxis cruising the streets of Manhattan.

The driver was reluctant to drive to Queens, but Russ gave him a fifty-dollar bill and promised him another one when he took them to the airport. He explained that the driver would have to wait at the company they were going to. If it was longer than five minutes, he'd pay even more.

Isabella's eyes were wide at his generosity. ''You could've gotten him for less,'' she whispered.

''I want to be sure he's waiting for us. I don't want you to worry about anything. It's all going to be fine.''

When they arrived at the factory her father ran, the man at the gate wasn't going to let them in. Isabella leaned forward. ''Hello, Mike. It's me, Isabella Paloni, only I'm married now. We just want to see my father for a few minutes.''

''Miss Isabella! Yeah, sure, sorry, I didn't see you.''

He waved them through.

''Your dad runs a tight ship.''

''Very tight,'' Isabella murmured.

At the large entrance, the cabbie turned and looked at them. ''I wait longer than five minutes and I get more money?''

''Exactly. Just be here when we come out.

You've got our luggage in your trunk,'' Russ reminded him.

''Will do, pal.''

''I feel better knowing we have our escape planned,'' Isabella whispered to Russ. This time, she initiated their handholding, which pleased him.

Isabella indicated the executive offices. ''My brother's is the office on the left. Dad's is on the right.''

The woman guarding the entrance to both offices looked up. ''Miss Paloni. May I help you?''

''I'd like to see my father—at once, please.''

Russ was proud of her. He knew she was scared, because he could feel her hand trembling in his. But she held her head up and kept her voice calm.

''I'm sorry. He's in a meeting and—''

''Interrupt him. Or I will.''

''Well…well, all right. Just a minute.'' The woman picked up the phone and spoke in a low voice. They could hear enough to realize her father refused to see her.

''Your father said for you to go home. He'll talk to you tonight.''

Russ stepped to the door on the right and opened it. The two of them entered.

''Who are you?'' Isabella's father demanded.

Russ could see the similarities between father and daughter, but Isabella showed no signs of the meanness on the man's face. ''I'm your daughter's husband, Russ Randall. We won't take much of your time, but we're on a tight schedule.''

"I don't have time for social visits. I don't care who she married this time. She's out of my life."

Russ smiled. "That's the way I want it, too."

Isabella stepped forward. "Dad, I wanted to tell you face-to-face what I've done with the stock."

"You have it?" he asked tightly.

"Yes, Great-aunt Maria left it to me. But I don't want any part of your company, so I've sold the stock. A competitor bought it all and is planning a hostile takeover. I realize it will affect your control. So I thought you should know."

"By the way," Russ added casually, "I wouldn't do any traveling in Wyoming, if I were you. You might not ever get back to New York." Then he and Isabella walked out, leaving a dumbfounded Antonio Paloni staring after them.

Isabella laughed with relief as they got back into the taxi.

Russ leaned forward. "Let's go."

When the cab reached the company gate, the driver waved to the guard and he waved back, and then they were through. Russ looked over his shoulder and saw the guard pick up the phone and try to wave them back. He said nothing to Isabella.

"We did it!" she declared. "Your threat was wonderful! The perfect threat! Oh, Russ, thank you for helping me face him. I feel very good about that."

"I'm glad you do, honey. You were very brave."

"Because you were there with me," she told him with a beautiful smile.

"I'm your husband. We work together. I expect you to protect me when some woman hits on me."

He was teasing, but Isabella took his words seriously. "I will," she promised.

He liked the thought of Izzy fighting off other women. It pleased him that she agreed they were a team. One he could rely on for the rest of his life. He intended to hold her and Angel close. It had even occurred to him that they might give Angel a brother or sister. A delicious, but scary thought.

When they got to the airport a few minutes later, Russ tipped the driver generously. The man's gratitude embarrassed Russ, but Isabella laughed. "Next time we come to New York, I'd better be in control of the tipping. Otherwise we'll have taxis following us around to see if we want a ride."

"If it's raining, it might be worth it," Russ drawled.

"You've been to New York before?" she asked curiously.

"Abby and I were here for our honeymoon. She wanted to see the Big Apple once."

Immediately Isabella sobered. "Oh, I'm sorry. I didn't know. I should've come alone."

"I'm your husband, Izzy. Don't forget that. It's my job to protect you." He picked up their two suitcases. "Let's go get checked in. The lines will probably be long."

Their plane took off two hours later. They'd had lunch at one of the restaurants in the terminal. Once they were settled on the plane, Isabella fell asleep, exhausted, apparently, by the morning's confrontation.

Russ took out his credit card and initiated a long-distance call to the ranch.

"Red, it's Russ. Is Dad there?"

"He sure is, boy. He's been pacing the floor."

"Russ? Is everything all right?" Pete asked a moment later.

"Everything's fine. Isabella was terrific. Her father was too surprised to even say anything."

"Wonderful. We've been worried. Your brother is here." He handed over the phone.

"Russ? Why didn't you take me with you?" Rich demanded. "You know I would've watched your back."

"Sometimes a man has to stand up for his woman by himself, Rich. But thanks for the offer."

"You're on the plane?"

"Yes. New York is a speck on the ground below. Izzy's asleep. We didn't get much last night. We'll get to Denver about five. Then we'll catch the next flight to Casper. Can someone meet the plane?"

"Sam and I will. We can have dinner in Casper when we pick you up. Gram will watch our baby."

"That sounds good. How's Jack?"

"Hurting from the sheriff's lecture more than the wound. He'll be on his feet in a few days."

"Good. Okay, we'll look for you in Casper," Russ said. "Tell Dad I appreciate his concern."

"If you talked to Mom, you wouldn't say that. She's been driving us all crazy."

"I hoped Angel would keep her busy."

He could hear the grin in Rich's voice. "It'll take more than one baby to do that. She raised twins, remember?"

"Yeah. I'll have to see what I can do about that."

RUSS DIDN'T SLEEP at all on the plane. All he could think about was the future, his and Izzy's future. Would she stay with him? Could he continue to share a bed with her and not make love to her? Would she ever want him the way he wanted her?

He had no answers. He'd promised to wait a year. He was an idiot! He would be out of his mind if he slept beside her an entire year but didn't make love to her. But he'd promised.

When they got off the plane in Casper, his twin and Samantha were waiting for them. "I hope you're starving," Rich said, a grin on his face, "because I am. We found a good restaurant right on the edge of town as we came in. Is that okay with you two?"

"Oh, yes, that would be wonderful," Isabella said. "I'm hungry, too. Did you go by and check on Angel before you left?"

"We stopped by," Samantha said, "but it was to ask Pete and Janie if they wanted to come with us. Janie had Angel in her arms, talking to her. She seemed very happy."

"Mom or Angel?" Russ asked.

"Both of them," returned Samantha.

Isabella smiled. ''Good. Then we've got time to eat.''

They settled into a booth at the restaurant and discovered a varied menu. Isabella ordered a barbecue sandwich with fries. Russ stared at her.

''I didn't know you liked barbecue.''

''I didn't know I did either until I moved out here. They don't serve it in New York.''

''What else is different from New York?'' Samantha asked.

Isabella laughed. ''The availability of cabs. I haven't seen any in Wyoming. And delivery of food. In New York you can order food by phone and it will be there in fifteen minutes and still be warm.''

''You mean pizza?'' Samantha asked.

''Any kind of food. For any meal. You can order breakfast.''

''I didn't know that. But we're so spread out here.'' Samantha looked at her husband. ''I might like to go to New York for a visit someday.''

''Are you homesick?'' Russ asked Isabella warily.

''A little,'' she said.

Russ worried about the homesickness growing.

''But we'll be home in two hours, so I guess I can wait,'' Isabella added.

Russ froze. Then he looked at his wife. ''You mean you're homesick for Wyoming?''

''Not Wyoming exactly, but Rawhide. It's a neat little town, full of good people.''

"I thought you meant you were homesick for New York." Russ took her hand in his.

She squeezed his fingers. "No. I don't have good memories of New York. But my time in Rawhide has been full of good experiences." She paused, then added, "Even the blizzard was exciting, from what I can remember. And everything turned out all right because you came along and rescued us."

"That's kind of like my driving Rich home when he hurt his ankle. I didn't intend to fall for him, but then we both moved to his grandmother's ranch and I couldn't help falling in love with him. In the end, it turned out all right," Samantha said with a big smile. "In fact, it turned out so right that we're expecting another baby." Her cheeks were bright red.

Rich put his arm around his wife and smiled, too, a satisfied look on his face.

"Congratulations," Russ said. "Are you hoping for a girl this time?"

"I'm hoping for twins," Rich said.

"I'm not," Samantha protested. "I don't think I can manage two babies at once."

"It sounds tough, but I'll help you if you have twins," Isabella promised.

"Or you could have another baby, too," Rich suggested.

Now it was Isabella's turn to blush.

Russ said, "Angel is only two months old. I think Izzy would like more time not being pregnant. There's no rush."

"That's true, especially since Angel already has cousins to play with," Samantha said.

The waitress brought their food and Russ drew a deep breath of relief. "Here's our food. We'd better concentrate on eating so we can reunite Izzy and Angel. Mom may be getting tired of baby-sitting."

That drew laughs from Rich and Samantha, but they all began eating.

When they reached the ranch, Izzy had a joyful reunion with her daughter, with Russ hanging over her shoulder. They both swore Angel smiled at them.

"It was probably gas," Janie said. "That's what my mother told me when the boys smiled."

"Hey, Mom, we have some news for you," Rich said.

Russ was surprised when he felt Izzy take his hand. She knew what was coming. Did it upset her? He figured she was thinking about Rich and Samantha's suggestion she have another baby right away, but surely she knew he wouldn't pressure her. Hell, he hadn't even made love to her yet.

There was general celebrating over their good news and Russ and Izzy's return. Then Russ encouraged Izzy to pack Angel's things so they could return to their apartment. Red had packed a box of food for them. "So you can have breakfast in the morning without going out."

Russ grinned at Izzy. "See, honey, we have delivery here, too."

"It's true," she said. "And the food here tastes better."

"Of course it does." Red grinned.

"Is there a chocolate cake in that box?" Russ asked.

"Sure is. Chocolate cake is good for you."

"I think you're right. Izzy sure likes it," Russ told Red, as Isabella blushed again.

"That's a good sign for other things, liking chocolate," Red said. When the others shushed Red, Russ figured it had something to do with sex.

He loaded the box of groceries and Angel's things in the back of Rich's truck. When they got to town, Rich helped carry their belongings upstairs. Izzy invited them up for some cake before they went home, but they were anxious to get back to their child.

Russ walked his brother out to his truck with a thank-you for picking them up. When he came back in, Izzy was unpacking the food. She put the fresh eggs in the refrigerator and the loaf of bread in the pantry. There was some milk that she left on the counter.

"I want some milk with my cake," she said. "Do you, Russ?"

"Yes, please." He stepped into the spare bedroom to check on Angel. She'd drifted back to sleep during the ride home.

When he returned to the living room, Izzy had cut a couple of slices of chocolate cake and was pouring the milk. "I wasn't sure what they were saying about the chocolate cake, but it doesn't matter. I really love it. I think eating chocolate keeps you happy."

"I think they were trying to say you're a passionate woman," Russ said, not meeting her gaze. "But I have no complaints."

Chapter Seventeen

They enjoyed their cake and milk. Russ watched as Izzy licked the last bit of chocolate icing off her fork. "Want another piece?" he asked.

"I'd love one, but I can't have it. I'll wait until tomorrow, or I'll look like a float in the Macy's Thanksgiving parade."

"I have a confession to make before you go to bed."

"A confession? What could it be?"

"I lied to you in New York."

"What about?"

He thought he saw fear in her eyes. "I didn't want you to be upset. But someone sent a man here to help the two criminals escape."

"They escaped?"

"Yeah. The man shot the deputy, too."

"And he's dead? Oh, no! How awful! No one will want me to stay here after that. I'm going to have to leave Rawhide." Isabella covered her face with her hands.

''Hey, the deputy didn't die. He's going to get well. And it's partly his fault anyway. He let the man in without searching either him or his brief-case.''

''He shouldn't have to die because he got a little careless,'' she protested.

''In that line of work, you'd better not be care-less. The sheriff let him have it when he was sta-bilized. And there'll be no leaving, Izzy. You prom-ised forever. Remember?''

''I remember. But Russ, you can't want me to stay. I'm glad I was able to help you get over your mourning, but you can't want a life with me. I bring trouble.''

''Your father brought trouble. But I think we've heard the last of him.''

''But Angel has his blood. What if she takes after him?''

Isabella asked, tears streaming down her cheeks. He drew her into his arms and held her there even when she tried to push away.

''I don't think Angel will do that. Especially since she's going to live here, with you and me. We'll teach her the right things.''

''I think it would be better if Angel and I dis-appeared. You deserve better than me.''

''You're overly tired. Let's get some rest. We've got plenty of time to discuss our future.'' He pulled her to her feet and led her into the bedroom. He dug out another pajama top and told her to take the bathroom first. In no time, they were tucked into the big bed. As Isabella began to succumb to her exhaustion, Russ slipped his arms around her and drew her close.

"Russ," she whispered, her voice slurring, "Don't let me go. I might get lost."

"I won't let you go, honey. You're here to stay, you and Angel."

THE NEXT DAY Russ returned to work, and Isabella decided to do some more shopping. A lot of Angel's wardrobe was burned in the fire, also. Isabella was constantly washing to keep Angel in clean clothes.

She called Sarah and asked her to join her on another shopping trip. It was more fun with Sarah along. After an hour of buying baby clothes, Sarah suggested they visit the café for coffee and maybe something to eat.

"I get hungry about ten o'clock. I'm hoping it's the pregnancy," Sarah said. "Otherwise, I'll still weigh a ton after I have the baby."

"I'm sure it's the pregnancy. I ate everything in sight when I was pregnant and I've returned to my regular weight."

"I know. I'm so jealous," Sarah said with a laugh. "You are going to have a cinnamon bun, aren't you?"

"I guess. I've got chocolate cake at home, though."

"You can eat that later," Sarah suggested, grinning.

The waitress arrived. ''Hello, ladies. So, Mrs. Randall, you're back?''

Since she was looking at her, Isabella knew the woman was talking to her. Besides, everyone called Sarah by her first name. ''You sure do have an effect on the town,'' the waitress went on. ''Rawhide used to be calm. Now we have murder and mayhem because of you.''

Isabella was horrified. The town blamed her? Now she knew she had to leave. She couldn't saddle Russ with the burden of her reputation. Soon they'd start blaming *him* for keeping her here. She lowered her eyes, staring at her clasped hands on the table.

Sarah didn't wait for the waitress to continue her conversation. ''I don't think that's Izzy's fault. Bring us coffee and a cinnamon roll each.'' She turned to Izzy when the waitress left. ''Don't pay any attention to what that woman said. She's probably thrilled with all the excitement. It's not your fault.''

''I'm afraid it is, Sarah. And I can't promise it won't happen again.''

''If it does happen again, we'll deal with it, just like we did this time. You're a part of our family now.''

Isabella tried to hide her concern. There was no point in upsetting Sarah. She needed to stay calm and happy for her baby. ''You sure have a good stock of baby clothes, Sarah. I think I got everything Angel needs.''

"I'm glad. I don't have to worry about the stock not moving. The Randalls are keeping us supplied with customers, my sister in particular."

"Did you know Rich and Samantha are expecting again?"

"No!" Sarah exclaimed, pleased about the news. "That will be someone for my child to play with. That's nice."

"Won't the twins play with your baby?"

"Yes, of course, but they're a year older. Christmas next year is going to be wild, isn't it? Angel will be walking and talking by then."

"Yes, she will." She'd be old enough to cry if Izzy took her away, too. Better she do so before Angel was old enough to notice. If it wasn't already too late. She was pretty sure Angel would miss Russ when they went away. She knew *she* would. But she didn't want to think about that. If she did, she'd start crying.

She and Angel returned to the store with Sarah for another hour and Isabella picked out a few more things for herself. She bought another suitcase to match the one she'd taken to New York. Then she invited Sarah back to their place for lunch.

"I need to check with Nick," Sarah said.

"He can come, too. We're just having sandwiches."

"Oh, that would be fun. I'll go home and check with him. Then I'll give you a call."

"Okay. Thanks for shopping with me."

"Any time. I enjoy it."

Isabella didn't look in on Russ before going upstairs. She needed to think. The waitress's words had upset her. She'd actually thought yesterday on the plane that she could have a new life here with Russ. But not if staying made his life worse.

He'd been so good to her and Angel, taking care of her when she was sick, marrying her and standing beside her to face her father. And now she repaid him by disturbing the peace and quiet of Rawhide.

But how could she leave? It wasn't just Angel who would miss Russ. She'd never known a man like him. He was gentle and kind, loving and patient, brave and strong. And she loved his touch. She'd seriously considered telling him she didn't want him to wait a year before he made love to her.

She knew he'd keep his promise. He was that kind of man. But sleeping with him if she wasn't going to stay would only make matters worse. Besides, so far she hadn't figured out what was so wonderful about sex. Her first husband hadn't convinced her. Maybe she was frigid.

Sarah called to say she and Nick would join them for lunch. She offered to bring some potato salad to go with the sandwiches. Isabella gladly accepted the offer. That was one of the wonderful things here in Rawhide. Everyone pitched in. Of course, most of them were Randalls!

By the time Nick and Sarah came upstairs, along with Russ, Isabella had the table set and had sandwich makings laid out on the kitchen counter. They all made their own sandwiches and then gathered at the table where they could add potato salad to their plates.

They discussed family news and other goings-on in Rawhide, steering away from Isabella's problems. She figured Russ had asked their friends to avoid that topic. While she was grateful, it only made her all the more aware of how much she had disturbed the peace of Rawhide.

After lunch Russ said he was dropping by the hospital to give Jack, the deputy who'd been shot, a book to read. "Want to go with me, Izzy? I don't think you've met Jack Hayes."

"Are you sure he'll want to see me?" she asked.

"Of course he will."

"Go," Sarah said. "I'll stay here with Angel. In fact, I might take a nap along with her."

"Oh, Sarah, that's so nice of you."

Nick left with Russ and Izzy. "Thanks for letting Sarah care for Angel. It builds her confidence about handling a new baby."

"She's wonderful to offer so much. She's such a good friend." His words made her feel much better about her visit to the hospital. Maybe Russ was right and the deputy wouldn't blame her.

Jack seemed happy to see Russ. "Hey, Russ, thanks for coming by."

"I thought you might like a good murder mystery, since you have to stay in bed for a while."

"That's terrific," Jack said, reaching for the

book. Then his gaze fell on Isabella. ‘‘Who’s the good-looking lady?’’

‘‘Oh, sorry, Jack, this is my wife, Isabella. I forgot you hadn’t met her.’’

‘‘She’s the one those two men tried to burn? That means she’s the reason I almost died. Lady, you’re causing a lot of trouble around here.’’ His face was screwed up in a ferocious frown.

Izzy was shocked by his vehemence. She’d thought he might consider her responsible, but not as much as he apparently did.

‘‘Whoa, Jack,’’ Russ said. ‘‘That’s not Izzy’s fault. Blame the criminals if you want, but not Izzy.’’

‘‘I will, too, blame her. She almost cost me my life, and maybe my job, too.’’

‘‘The sheriff is going to fire you?’’ Izzy asked, appalled.

‘‘Haven’t decided yet,’’ a gruff voice behind them said. They both spun around to find an older, grizzled man with a badge on his shirt. ‘‘But whether I do or not has nothing to do with this young lady, Jack. You didn’t follow procedure. That’s what cost you that bullet.’’

‘‘Aw, Sheriff, I told you I was almost asleep,’’ Jack whined.

‘‘No excuses. You should have slept, instead of running around all day. You knew you had night duty.’’ His voice changed from stern to friendly as he turned to Isabella. ‘‘Ma’am, I haven’t met you, but I’m sure glad to welcome you to Rawhide.’’

"Oh, please, I'm sorry. I didn't mean to cause so much trouble."

"It wasn't you I arrested, so I don't reckon that's your fault."

"That's very generous of you, Sheriff," she said, but she didn't see any agreement in Jack's expression. She backed toward the door, glad when Russ followed her after saying goodbye to the two men.

In the hallway he caught up with her and put an arm around her shoulders. "Jack was wrong, honey. Don't pay any attention to what he said."

"No, of course not. The sheriff was very nice."

"Yeah, he's a good guy. I'm afraid he's going to retire soon. Not sure what we'll do then."

"Russ, is my car all right? It was in the garage and no one has said—"

"I'm sorry, honey, I should've told you. The engine still works, but the paint was singed and the inside reeks of smoke. Do you want it?"

"No. No, I don't. I guess I'll get another car."

"Sure. We can go shopping for one whenever you want. They have several dealerships in Buffalo. You might think about a SUV this time—for those winter storms," he added, winking at her.

"Yes, good idea." She smiled at him, trying to hide her worry. "You might not come along next time."

They reached the door. But before she could step outside, he took both her hands in his. "I'll always be there for you and Angel. You can count on that, honey."

She swallowed the tears that were building. She couldn't cry here, now. "That's a wonderful promise, Russ." She leaned forward to give him a little kiss, as he'd been giving her the past few days. But Russ wrapped his arms around her and took that little kiss to a major kiss.

"I see your snow maiden has completely recovered," Dr. Jon Wilson said behind them. Izzy's face turned bright red.

"Yeah, she's thawed out," Russ said with a chuckle. Izzy tried to smile at Russ's joke.

"Good, good. Is Tori still at the office?"

"She said she was going home at two," Russ said, looking at his watch.

"Good. I want her to take some time off this week. I figure there isn't a lot of business transacted around the holidays," Jon said.

"Just mine," Izzy muttered. She guessed she was messing up Tori's vacation, as well as the other problems she'd created.

After saying goodbye to Jon, they buttoned up their coats and walked outside. "A brisk walk in this cold air ought to make you want to join Angel for a nap, too," Russ said as they headed along the sidewalk.

"Yes," she said simply.

"Are you all right?" Russ asked, leaning down to see her face, ducked into the collar of her coat.

"Just cold."

"You're not still bothered by what Jack said, are you? If you are, we'll go back to the hospital and

I'll point out whose fault it was. He really did a sloppy job."

"But it was unexpected."

"There are some jobs that can't tolerate sloppiness. His is one of them." He hugged her closer as they hurried the two blocks to the apartment.

Isabella didn't say anything else until they got there. Then she said, "Can we go into Buffalo tomorrow to buy me a SUV? I don't know anything about them. Do you?"

"Yeah. I'll show you the ones I like. It'll be fun. Can you get Sarah to keep Angel tomorrow?"

"Oh, I hate to ask her again tomorrow. Can't we take Angel with us?"

"It would be hard on her. I'll call Mom and see if we can drop her off at the ranch."

"Are you sure she won't mind? She might want to go out."

"Mom loves Angel. And it's winter. She seldom goes out to work during the winter. There isn't all that much to do when it's this cold out."

"All right. But call her from downstairs so she won't worry about me hearing if she needs to turn us down."

"Sure. I'll call her as soon as I get in." Then he kissed her again.

She sure was getting used to his special kisses.

Chapter Eighteen

They returned from Buffalo the next afternoon. Isabella proudly drove her new SUV and parked it near the back door at the ranch so everyone could see it.

She loved it. But she didn't love what it represented. It was her means of leaving Russ. Of leaving the Randall family. She'd made so many friends here. She'd discovered love, love of family, love of friends and love of a man. She was going to really miss Russ. Doing anything with him was fun. He made it so. Leaving him was going to be very hard.

She knew she'd have to make plans at once. Any delay would only make her departure more difficult.

Everyone admired the SUV. Then Red asked them to stay for dinner, to which they readily agreed. Janie called Rich and Samantha and asked them to come over for dinner, too. Izzy was pleased that she'd be able to see everyone one more time, but the thought was bittersweet.

Janie grinned at her. "Life is so much better

these days, Izzy. It's wonderful to see Russ happy again. I give thanks every day for your coming here.''

''That's more than most of the people in Rawhide do,'' she said, and then instantly wished she could take the words back.

Janie suddenly looked grim.

''Just tell me who made you feel that way. I'll deal with them,'' she said.

''No, no, Janie, I didn't mean...it's no big deal,'' Izzy said.

''This is your home now. Forever.''

''I know, Janie, thanks to you and Pete and all the rest of the family. You've all been so nice to me and Angel.''

''It's not hard to be nice to you or Angel, my dear.''

''Thank you, Janie.'' Isabella smiled at her new mother-in-law.

RUSS EXCUSED HIMSELF and went to the barn. He remained there until his brother and Samantha arrived.

''Hey, Russ, what are you doing out here?'' Rich called as he got out of his truck.

''I need to talk to you. Do you mind, Samantha?''

''No, of course not. I'll go visit with Izzy.''

The two brothers stood together until Russ heard the back door close. Then Rich turned to Russ. ''What's up?''

"I think Izzy is going to leave me."

"What?" Rich shouted, "No, she can't! You two've been so happy. You mustn't—"

"Don't worry. I don't intend to let her."

"You're going to talk her out of it?"

"Nope. That won't work. She's being noble. She thinks she's doing the right thing for me."

"How does she figure that?"

"A couple of people in town have made remarks about all the trouble she's brought Rawhide. And she believed them."

"Did you tell her it's not her fault?"

Russ gave his brother a look of disgust. "Of course I told her. She wanted to know if her car was drivable."

"Is it?"

"Yeah, but it's nasty because of the fire. So we went to Buffalo today and bought her a new SUV."

"Wow, so that's her SUV? I wondered who'd bought that."

"Yeah. I think she's planning on loading in Angel and their clothes and hitting the road."

Rich shook his head. "I remember when Sam got on that bus. If Doc hadn't seen her there and called, I might have lost her. So what are you going to do?"

"Well, number one, I'm going to watch her like a hawk. And number two, I'm going to siphon out most of her gas. She won't think to look because she just filled it today. She'll get a couple of miles out of town and run out. And I'll be right behind her."

"But if she really wants to run away, you can't watch her every minute."

"She doesn't want to."

"Are you sure?"

"Yeah. She thinks we're a unique family: Unique in our niceness. She's trying to be as nice as we are by leaving."

"That sounds kind of crazy to me," Rich said, scratching his head.

"Why was Samantha trying to leave you?"

"She didn't think I'd love her forever, and she didn't want to get pregnant and then have to move on."

"Well, I don't think that's true of Izzy. I honestly think she believes she owes me for being so good to her. She doesn't understand how marriage works, because she had such a lousy one for an example. I suspect she thinks she's frigid."

"Is she?"

"No," Russ said with a sweet smile on his face. "She's just scared."

"Maybe showing her would be better than draining her gas tank."

"Maybe. But I promised. So I can't."

"Man, this is crazy. Could Mom talk to her?"

"Nope. This is the only way. Just help me siphon the gas. I'll take care of the rest."

WHEN THE EVENING at the ranch wound down, Russ walked Izzy to her new vehicle. "You sure you're up to driving it?"

"Of course I am."

"Well, you start out and I'll follow right behind," he suggested.

"I don't need you to tail me. I can manage just fine."

"I'm sure you can, honey, but humor me. Dad taught us to take care of our women."

She gave him a disgusted look and reached for Angel, whom he'd carried from the house.

"I'll take Angel with me," he said. "That way you can concentrate on the driving."

"Really, Russ, I'll be fine."

"Better safe than sorry. Besides, the baby carrier's in the truck, remember? You'd have to switch it. So look, I'll see you at home." With Angel still in his arms, he walked over to his truck.

She slammed the door of her SUV a little more forcefully than necessary. Russ grinned. "I think Mommy is a little ticked off at me, Angel. But you still love me, don't you?"

Angel cooed at him and he grinned. "Mommy is going to get even more upset when she tries to run away. But don't worry. I'll be along to rescue you, okay?"

He hoped Izzy would understand as easily as Angel.

AFTER THEY GOT Angel settled in bed, Russ turned on the television and started watching an old movie he liked. Izzy went into the bedroom. He called for her to come watch the movie with him, but she said she was busy.

He peeked in the bedroom a few minutes later to discover her packing. He thought about confronting her then and there, but decided it wouldn't be effective. He'd wait until she made her move.

He did a lot of yawning and stretching when he went to bed an hour or so later. She was already under the covers. "You've gone to bed already?"

"Yes. I thought I could get a head start on Angel. She'll be up in a few hours."

"True. But I'll get up with her tonight. You had a long day today."

"No!"

From the alarm in her voice he realized she planned to leave in the middle of the night. Well, he'd foil that plan. "It's no problem. I'll feed her."

"No. I insist on feeding her. I'm missing a lot of things lately. She's not even going to know me if I'm not careful."

"You silly girl. Okay, you can feed her."

He kissed her cheek and crawled into bed with her.

When Angel woke them around four, Izzy scrambled out of bed. "You go back to sleep," she insisted.

He didn't say anything.

As soon as she'd gotten Angel and gone to the living room, he got out of bed and pulled on his jeans. Then he sauntered into the living room. "I can't seem to go back to sleep."

Izzy jumped. Clearly he'd startled her. "Sorry, I didn't mean to wake you," he said with a chuckle. "Want me to take her?"

"No, I can manage. If you tried I'm sure you could go back to sleep."

"But I'm hungry. I'm going to have a piece of cake. You want one?"

"No. You'll never get to sleep if you eat chocolate."

"Sure I will. Sure you won't have some?"

"No, I—yes, I'll have one. With a glass of milk."

He grinned at her and cut two generous pieces of Red's chocolate cake. Then he poured two glasses of milk. "Come on over to the table. You can eat while feeding her."

She did as he said. She ate her piece quickly, drinking her milk as she went. When Angel had finished her bottle, she burped her and then got up to put her in bed.

Russ sat there watching Izzy's frustration. He felt badly about tricking her, but no way was he going to let her get out on the highway in the middle of the night.

After she went back to bed, he waited another fifteen minutes, even though he was very sleepy. When he reentered the bedroom, the first thing he did was turn off the alarm. They could use a little extra sleep come morning. Then he climbed into bed and drew her against him. He loved holding her. And he'd love making love to her, too. As soon as he convinced her to stay.

WHEN IZZY AWOKE, she discovered first of all that her body was plastered against Russ's. She immediately shifted away, even though she didn't want to. Unfortunately her movement woke him.

"Russ, I think the alarm must've gone off. What time is it?"

He stretched, then looked at the clock. "Yeah, it was set to go off a couple of hours ago, but I turned it off after you fed Angel. I thought we deserved a little extra sleep this morning."

"So what time is it?" she repeated sharply.

"Nine-thirty. Ready to get up?"

"Oh, my, yes. I meant to— I shouldn't get used to sleeping this late."

"I don't think Angel will let you. But I think her feeding schedule is changing. Mom said we start cereal at three months, so we might get her sleeping all night pretty soon."

"Yes, um, that's true."

"We fed her at four, so she should be up in another half hour. If you want a shower before you feed her, you'd better get a move on."

He watched as she looked guiltily at the closet where her packed suitcases were hidden. She had planned to leave much earlier without a shower. He took pity on her. "I'll go put on a pot of coffee. Want me to make pancakes?"

"No, thank you. I'm not hungry."

Angel was fed and breakfast eaten before he got ready to go to work. He kissed Izzy goodbye and thumped down the stairs. Instead of going into his office, he went into the newspaper office next door. He offered a reward to the young man who worked there if he notified him as soon as he saw Izzy drive off in her SUV. He could see it from the window.

Then Russ went to his office and started to work, but he was easily distracted. Any minute he expected his spy to report that Izzy had left.

At noon he stepped outside to be sure the SUV was there. There it sat in all its glory…and a few snowflakes. Were they in for a storm?

He hurried up the stairs. Izzy was vacuuming the floor. When he tapped her on her shoulder, she practically jumped out of her shoes.

"Hi, sweetheart. You're working hard. Sure you feel up to it?"

"Yes, I do. Did you know we're going to have another snowstorm?"

"No, I didn't. Did you watch the weather channel?"

"Yes. There's a storm moving in over the Rockies. They think it will start snowing this afternoon."

"Ah. I think it's already started. Is that why you haven't run away yet?"

His words made her turn off the vacuum cleaner and sit down at the table. "You knew?"

"Yeah. I figured."

"I'll go as soon as the snow ends. I think we both know I'm not a good driver in the snow. I don't want to endanger Angel. But I will go, I promise."

"And you think I'll be happy about that?"

"Maybe not at first, but in the long run, you'll be glad I'm not here to cause any more trouble in Rawhide." By the time she finished, her lower lip was trembling.

"You silly girl," he said tenderly. "The only thing that will cause any more trouble is you leaving."

When he held out his arms to her, she fell into them, tears streaming down her face. "I have to leave, Russ. People are irritated that I upset the calm of Rawhide."

"Do you think I care about what anyone says about Rawhide's peace? My peace would be destroyed if you and Angel left."

"I don't want to go, Russ," Izzy cried, sobbing.

"Then don't."

"But I won't make you a good wife. I've already been married once. I didn't make him happy."

"Ah. Now we're talking about sex, aren't we?" he guessed.

"I know you agreed no sex. But you're right. You can't live forever without sex. And I can't expect you to, but I'd die if you had another woman."

"So would I, because you're the only woman I want."

"But I can't…I mean, I didn't—"

He kissed her, then wiped away her tears. "Listen, honey, I promised I'd wait a year." He sighed. "Sweetheart, sex with me will be different. And if you don't like it, we'll do whatever you think is right."

"You mean...you want to have sex now? I'll disappoint you, I know it."

"I don't think so." He smiled at her. "If you hate the idea so much, why do you let me hold you at night?"

"Because it's cold?" she tried weakly.

He took her by the hand. "Come on, Izzy. Let's give it a try."

"But the baby..."

"Did you feed her at ten?"

"Ten-thirty, actually."

"Then she won't wake up until five or so. Perfect timing."

He led her to the bedroom. Sitting down on the edge of the bed, he pulled her into his lap. The first kiss was a delight. But Izzy was still tense, as if waiting for something bad to happen. Russ continued to kiss her. Gradually she began to respond, became as eager and hungry as he was.

Soon they were stretched out on the bed. He unbuttoned her blouse enough that he could occasionally drop a kiss on her warm skin, but he made no attempt to remove her clothes.

Finally she sat up and gave him a puzzled frown. "Is there something wrong with me?"

"Nothing at all," he replied.

''Look, I know we have to get naked. Are you afraid you'll shock me? Because I...I want to.''

Russ smiled a big smile. ''Well, I'm ready. But I wanted to wait until you were.''

''I like kissing you,'' she volunteered.

''Good. I like kissing you. Shall I help you undress?''

She looked alarmed again. ''No, I can manage.''

She headed for the bathroom. He stopped her. ''Honey, did your husband send you to the bathroom to get undressed?''

She nodded.

''Then did he go to the bathroom to undress?'' When she nodded again, his eyebrows shot up. ''I'm afraid I'm going to shock you.''

''How?''

''I want to undress you and I want you to undress me. But there's no hurry. I want you to enjoy it.''

She looked as if that was a novel concept. ''Enjoy undressing?''

''Yeah. Come here and I'll show you.''

The next half hour was a revelation to Izzy. And Russ was right. She did enjoy it. So much so that she got a little impatient with his dillydallying....

In the end she found making love with Russ to be incredibly enjoyable, incredibly satisfying. So much so that she wondered what her first husband had been doing. It certainly wasn't making love.

When her trembling had stopped and she lay peacefully against his chest, he stroked her bare back and asked her if she was all right.

"All right? I'm feeling wonderful. Can we…can we do that again?"

Russ chuckled. "Now? It takes me a little while to recover, honey."

"How long?"

He laughed. "A couple of hours."

"Oh. I was afraid you would say a week. That's usually how often my first husband—"

"I think we need to wash him out of your memory. I don't think he was a good husband."

"Mmm, me, neither."

"So you're willing to stay as long as we do this a lot?"

Her cheeks flushed, but she met his glance. "Yes, but really, Russ, if you think I need to go, I will. I mean, I don't want to, but I don't want to ruin your life." She snuggled closer. "If it weren't for the snow, I would've been gone this morning."

"Not permanently."

"Yes, Russ, I was seriously going to leave."

"I know. But I wasn't going to seriously let you go."

"You wouldn't have known. I was all packed and everything."

"But you wouldn't get far."

"Why not?"

"Because I siphoned most of your gas out of the SUV."

She sat up, startled. He didn't think he'd ever seen anything as beautiful as Isabella at that moment, the covers gathered around her waist, her breasts full and rosy, her hair tumbling over her shoulders.

But her mind was on other matters. ''You did what?''

''I wanted to make sure I didn't lose you.''

''But that wasn't fair!''

He was still smiling, but his voice was serious. ''When it comes to you and Angel, sweetheart, fair isn't what matters. Holding the two of you close is what matters. I love you, and I love Angel, too. I want to share my life with you.''

''I love you, too, Russ. I didn't know men like you existed. I don't ever want to leave.''

''Good.'' He reached for her. ''You know, Izzy, you inspire me. I seem to have recovered faster than I thought.''

''Are you sure? I don't want to hurt you,'' she said, concern in her voice.

''The only way you could hurt me would be to leave, sweetheart. Don't ever leave,'' he said, pulling her back to his side, kissing her.

''No, Russ, I won't,'' she promised, wrapping her arms around his neck.

''Then we'll be happy forever, Izzy, my love.''

Start the New Year off regally with a two-book duo from

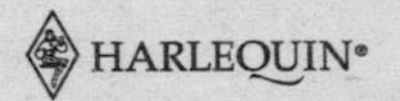

AMERICAN *Romance*®

A runaway prince and his horse-wrangling lookalike confuse and confound the citizens of Ranger Springs, Texas, in

by

Victoria Chancellor

Rodeo star Hank McCauley just happened to be a dead ringer for His Royal Highness Prince Alexi of Belegovia—who had just taken off from his tour of Texas with a spirited, sexy waitress. Now, Hank must be persuaded by the very prim-and-proper Lady Gwendolyn Reed to pose as the prince until the lost leader is found. But could she turn the cowpoke into a Prince Charming? And could Hank persuade Lady "Wendy" to let down her barriers so that he could have her, body and soul?

Don't miss:

THE PRINCE'S COWBOY DOUBLE
January 2003

Then read Prince Alexi's story in:

THE PRINCE'S TEXAS BRIDE
February 2003

Available at your favorite retail outlet.

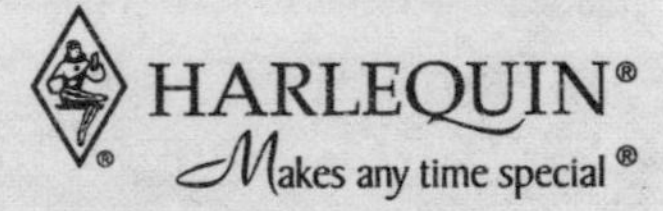

Visit us at www.eHarlequin.com

HARPCD